THE HE

BARBARA CARTLAND

Barbaracartland.com Ltd

.com

POD Preparation by M-Y Books
m-ybooks.co.uk

THE BARBARA CARTLAND PINK COLLECTION

Barbara Cartland was the most prolific bestselling author in the history of the world. She was frequently in the Guinness Book of Records for writing more books in a year than any other living author. In fact her most amazing literary feat was when her publishers asked for more Barbara Cartland romances, she doubled her output from 10 books a year to over 20 books a year, when she was 77.

She went on writing continuously at this rate for 20 years and wrote her last book at the age of 97, thus completing 400 books between the ages of 77 and 97.

Her publishers finally could not keep up with this phenomenal output, so at her death she left 160 unpublished manuscripts, something again that no other author has ever achieved.

Now the exciting news is that these 160 original unpublished Barbara Cartland books are ready for publication and they will be published by Barbaracartland.com exclusively on the internet, as the web is the best possible way to reach so many Barbara Cartland readers around the world.

The 160 books will be published monthly and will be numbered in sequence.

The series is called the Pink Collection as a tribute to Barbara Cartland whose favourite colour was pink and it became very much her trademark over the years.

The Barbara Cartland Pink Collection is published only on the internet. Log on to www.barbaracartland.com to find out how you can purchase the books monthly as they are published, and take out a subscription that will ensure that all subsequent editions are delivered to you by mail order to your home.

TITLES IN THIS SERIES

THE LATE DAME BARBARA CARTLAND

Barbara Cartland, who sadly died in May 2000 at the grand age of ninety eight, remains one of the world's most famous romantic novelists. With worldwide sales of over one billion, her outstanding 723 books have been translated into thirty six different languages, to be enjoyed by readers of romance globally.

Writing her first book "Jigsaw" at the age of 21, Barbara became an immediate bestseller. Building upon this initial success, she wrote continuously throughout her life, producing bestsellers for an astonishing 76 years. In addition to Barbara Cartland's legion of fans in the UK and across Europe, her books have always been immensely popular in the USA. In 1976 she achieved the unprecedented feat of having books at numbers 1 & 2 in the prestigious B. Dalton Bookseller bestsellers list.

Although she is often referred to as the "Queen of Romance", Barbara Cartland also wrote several historical biographies, six autobiographies and numerous theatrical plays as well as books on life, love, health and cookery. Becoming one of Britain's most popular media personalities and dressed in her trademark pink, Barbara spoke on radio and television about social and political issues, as well as making many public appearances.

In 1991 she became a Dame of the Order of the British Empire for her contribution to literature and her work for humanitarian and charitable causes.

Known for her glamour, style, and vitality Barbara Cartland became a legend in her own lifetime. Best remembered for her wonderful romantic novels and loved by millions of readers worldwide, her books remain treasured for their heroic heroes, plucky heroines and traditional values. But above all, it was Barbara Cartland's overriding belief in the positive power of love to help, heal and improve the quality of life for everyone that made her truly unique.

"Nothing can be more modern and up-to-date than love and fidelity between one man to one woman."

Barbara Cartland

CHAPTER ONE
1897

Lady Verena Rosslyn gazed at her reflection in the ornate French dressing table mirror and sighed. The image pleased her – a young, attractive, heart-shaped face framed by masses of dark hair, punctuated by a full mouth the colour of crushed strawberries.

As she searched her deep blue eyes, she noticed a certain wistfulness about them.

Of course, she always carried a degree of sadness within her heart, having lost her mother some six years ago when she was just fifteen but no, it was more than that.

There was a longing within the depths, but for what she could not say.

As she was musing over the possibilities, there came a sharp knocking at her bedroom door.

"Enter," she said in a voice that was soft and melodious. So like her mother's, as her father, the Earl of Bradchester, had often told her.

"His Lordship wishes to speak to you, my Lady." Violet her maid was standing in the doorway looking nervous, "and he says you are to come right away."

'I wonder what it is that Papa finds so pressing?' muttered Verena to herself, as she rose from the dressing table and smoothed down her hair. She liked to wear it loose even though her father had said that it was unseemly for a young woman of twenty-one. 'I do hope it is not bad news.'

She swept along the hall to the magnificent staircase of Rosslyn Hall.

The house had been in the family for generations but had barely changed during her lifetime. Her mother, as a young bride, had taken responsibility for the décor and had spared no expense in creating a comfortable home fit for a family.

Sadly, Verena was the only child and the house had remained the same as a tribute to her mother.

Verena stroked the brass beehive knob on the door of her father's study for a second and then knocked twice.

Opening the mahogany panelled door, she could see the Earl engrossed at his desk.

"You wanted to see me urgently, Papa?" she asked of the still handsome man in his fifties, sitting hunched over some papers.

"Ah, Verena, dearest. I wanted to let you know that I will be going to London to stay in our Hertford Street house for a while. There are some matters that require my attention."

Verena did not dare ask him what they might be. She knew that what her father did in his business life was no concern of hers.

"Don't look so worried," he continued kindly. "There is just one trifle that needs to be dealt with. And whilst I am in London, I thought I might visit my sister, Lady Armstrong, in Regent's Park. Her husband has been ill for some time and it would please her to see a friendly face."

"Papa, how long will you be gone for?"

Verena hated to be parted from her father like this. After her mother had died, he had slid into a deep depression for almost two years, and even now, there was the occasional day when he was silent and cold.

"You will surely become lonely in London without any company."

"I will have that aplenty, my dearest. There will be much to occupy me. Please do not worry about me. Now, tell me how you intend to spend your time whilst I am away. There is that fine, black stallion in the stables to exercise that I bought recently. I'll warrant that once you acquaint yourself with him, you will hardly notice I have gone."

"Oh, Papa, how can you say that," she cried, throwing herself to her knees at his feet.

Tenderly, he stroked Verena's soft dark hair and whispered,

"So like your mother – " in a voice that was choked with emotion.

"Now, leave me, I have preparations to make. I will be back before long and perchance I may bring a surprise for you."

Verena rose from her knees, her eyes shining.

"A new hat – please, Papa. Something in the latest French style."

"We will see, dearest, we will see. The time will fly, I promise you."

*

The Rosslyn estate stretched for many miles into the heart of the Hampshire countryside. It was rightly famous for its superb stables that housed several Arab racehorses amongst others. The Earl loved racing as much as he enjoyed hunting, pursuits he had returned to only recently after his long, dark days of mourning.

Verena ran through the courtyard to the stables – Barker the groom was walking slowly along leading an old bay mare.

"I see that Bess has just been groomed," commented Verena, smiling fondly with her hand outstretched towards the mare.

"Don't you be feeding 'er sugar lumps," grumbled Barker, who had been in the service of her mother long before she had wed. He had watched Verena grow from a toddler to the comely young lady who now stood in front of him.

"Is Jet ready?" enquired Verena eagerly.

She had taken the feisty beast out every day since her father's departure – she loved the challenge of controlling Jet's wilful personality and it took her mind off her father's absence.

In spite of a few brief but loving notes, she had received hardly any news of him. All she knew was that her aunt's husband was feeling much better and that she, Lady Armstong, had dragged the Earl out to many fine balls.

"Here, my Lady," said Barker, leading Bess away, "Roper will bring Jet out for you. Mind how you go now, that strong will of his would get the better of a man twice your size."

"Jet and I have become firm friends," answered Verena, confidently. "When Papa returns he will be most impressed with how I have learned to handle him."

4

Jet was indeed an exciting ride – he snorted and pawed the ground, whinnying shrilly, his teeth worrying at the bit.

Later, as Verena rode Jet to the top of the hill that overlooked the estate, she was once again filled with longing.

'I feel as if my life has yet to begin,' she told herself, as Jet strained at the reins. 'There is something missing that I really cannot find here, much as I love this place.'

Digging her heels hard into Jet's side, the magnificent stallion took off like the wind. Verena's long, dark hair streamed out behind her and the sun beat down on her back as the pair made their way across the fields back to the stables.

*

Arriving tired and dusty back at Rosslyn Hall, Verena was greeted by the sight of Barker, hobbling towards her and waving his arms.

"Barker, what is it?"

"It's my Lord, the Earl, he's back! He's been asking for you since midday. We thought of sending out for you, but none of us knew where you'd be – or how far away you'd got. Looks like this rascal took you through the old quarry judging by the look of you both."

Verena dismounted. True enough, her riding habit was covered in white dust. Her long, green skirt was now grey and she did not care to think what her hair or face must have looked like.

'Now I must find my father. How strange that he did not send word about his arrival today. I would have made sure that the Hall was spotless with everything just how he likes it. I do hope the maids have aired his bed.'

Verena hurried towards the house, banging her skirt as she ran, sending clouds of dust over the gravel. As she mounted the steps at the front of the hall, she noticed that two footmen were bringing in great piles of packages and suitcases.

'How curious,' said Verena to herself. 'Either Papa has been exceedingly generous buying gifts for me in London or he has returned with some visitors. Surely there is too much luggage for just one person?' She approached one of the footmen, desperate to know what was going on.

"Markyate, has his Lordship brought back visitors from London?"

"Sorry, my Lady, I couldn't say."

'This is a pretty puzzle indeed,' she mused, 'but I am sure that presently, I will find out the answer.'

Just then, Oakes the butler appeared in front of her.

"His Lordship wishes to see you in the drawing room, my Lady. He asked me to tell you as soon as you arrived back from your ride."

'Well, now we will solve this mystery. I do hope Papa is on his own, I would hate for anyone to see me in such disarray.'

Moving quickly towards the drawing room, Verena felt strangely nervous, almost as if she sensed a presentiment that something unpleasant was going to happen.

She opened the double doors and saw immediately that her father was standing with his back to her, gazing out of the window across the park.

"Papa – " she began, "it grieves me to greet you in such a dishevelled state, but had I known of your arrival, I would surely have returned from my ride much sooner."

As her father turned, his demeanour strangely stiff and uncomfortable, she was suddenly aware that there was another person in the room. Out of the corner of her eye she glimpsed a slight figure on the sofa by the fireplace.

"Ah, Verena, dearest. I am so pleased to see you. A month away from Rosslyn and you is a month too long. However, matters required attention."

The Earl seemed not to be himself. Verena could not take her eyes off him as she searched his face, fruitlessly, for some sign of affection.

He made a rough gesture in the direction of the sofa.

Verena followed his hand and saw that a woman, neither young nor old, with a wide, haughty face was ensconced there, wearing an expression of utter confidence.

Again, her father waved in the strange woman's direction.

"There is someone I wish you to meet."

Verena looked questioningly again at her father, an uncomfortable feeling spreading throughout her frame.

"This, dearest, is Lady Louisa Middleton-Jones, my new wife. I trust you will be most welcoming to her and will show her around Rosslyn Hall. It would please me greatly if you would now go and kiss your new stepmother."

Verena stared in utter disbelief at her father.

How could he do this – request that she act towards this woman as she would to only a dear relative!

The word, *stepmother*, sounded ominous to her. She had but one mother and she was in her grave. Blood pounded in her temples as she tried to remain calm.

"Papa, I will afford Lady Louisa the proper courtesies as befitting a guest in this house, but with the deepest respect, please do not ask me to behave as a daughter to a complete stranger."

The Earl's face grew deep red with anger.

"Do you defy me? It is a simple request, daughter. I wish you to make your stepmother feel welcome in my house. And if I choose to ask you to kiss her, then kiss her you will! Do not make me angry – I have brought her here to be as a mother to you and to provide me with an heir and you with brothers. She has done me the honour of becoming my wife and now you will do me the honour of complying with my wishes without further comment."

For a few seconds, Verena remained frozen to the spot. Never had her father spoken to her in this harsh fashion and she could not understand what possessed him.

As she slowly advanced towards the stranger her heart was full of silent fury.

Who was this woman who had turned her father's head so? And how dare she think she could take the place of her sweet, beloved mother!

Stiffly Verena bent down and kissed the proffered cheek. As she drew back, she could see a thinly veiled look of disgust in cold eyes as they travelled over Verena's dusty riding habit and face.

Finally, the new Countess spoke,

"My dear, I can see that you have sorely missed a mother's guiding hand. I have promised your father that I will look after you and give you good counsel. I can see that I have arrived just in time."

Verena stood erect, her proud head held high, her body shaking.

"Father, may I please be excused? I need to change."

The Earl nodded tersely, his face an expressionless mask.

Verena's eyes filled with tears as she pulled the drawing room doors behind her.

What was wrong with her father? Never, even in his darkest depths of misery, had he behaved towards her in such a cold fashion. He had become a stranger to her and was no longer her own dear Papa.

*

Verena's worst fears were soon confirmed over the course of the next few months.

The Countess was determined to make her mark on Rosslyn Hall.

"I shall turn this decrepit place into a Palace again," she had said loftily, as she tugged at the voluptuous, Italian silk curtains in the drawing room that Verena's mother had brought back from her honeymoon in Florence. "These awful things will be the first to be replaced."

Verena could only look on in horror. "But my mother bought those. She loved them."

"And I do not, so they must come down immediately. I cannot bear to look at them for one moment longer."

The destruction of everything that Verena loved continued apace.

Everything old went in favour of the sparkling new – even the Earl was dressing differently. He wore coloured cravats and had grown a moustache – all because his new Countess had told him that the fashionable men of London were sporting one.

Verena's only escape was her riding.

As soon as breakfast was over, she would slip out of the back door and run towards the stables where Barker or Roper would be waiting with Jet.

As she covered mile after mile on the sleek animal, she felt friendless and afraid.

If her father had turned his back on her in favour of his new wife, what could she do? Who could she turn to?

There had been conversations suddenly terminated when she walked in and doors being closed whenever she appeared – almost as if there was some terrible secret lurking within the walls of the house that she was not allowed to know.

Furthermore, the Countess dogged her every step, making comments and passing judgements on how Verena wore her hair, how she dressed and her pastimes.

Verena began to feel like a prisoner in her own home.

Then one day, Verena was on her way back from the stables when she noticed what resembled a pile of old curtains round by the kitchen dustbins. She sighed as she ran to investigate. Rather than throw the things out, she thought that maybe the Church fete would be glad of them.

'Why, these do not seem to be furnishings,' she said to herself, pulling at the mound of material.

Slowly the awful truth dawned on her as she pulled out one long silk glove, followed by a tangle of cloaks and gowns.

She could not prevent the sobs from bursting forth as she realised that these were not some discarded chattels, but her own dear mother's belongings.

'There can only be one person responsible for this,' she choked. 'And I think it is time that Papa knew what kind of woman he has married.'

Grabbing one of her mother's favourite gowns – a white, summer muslin trimmed with *broderie anglaise* – she marched straight to her father's study.

Her knees were trembling as she slowly opened the door without knocking. It was some moments before her father realised that she was there.

"What is it, what ails you? You are looking quite pale, dearest."

Verena held out the muslin dress.

"Papa, I found this in the dustbins near the kitchen along with the rest of my mother's gowns."

The Earl looked puzzled for a second and then a shadow of irritation passed over his face.

"Verena, your stepmother asked my permission to dispose of them and I concurred. It no longer pleases me to have them hanging in the wardrobe when I have a new wife to consider."

"But Papa –"

"Verena, your mother is dead and whilst she is forever in my heart, there is no place for sentimentality in Rosslyn Hall. I have lived in the shadows long enough. Your stepmother has full authority to do what she will with both the house and its contents, she is now its Mistress and I leave all domestic matters to her. That is the end of the matter."

Curling up the muslin dress into a ball, Verena tearfully left the study.

'Truly I am alone,' she said to herself as she threw herself on her bed upstairs. 'Oh, Mama darling, how I miss you! If you can hear me wherever you are, please help me!' Verena cried herself to sleep and was only woken by Violet standing over her.

"My Lady, dinner is in ten minutes! I've been knocking for ages and you didn't hear me."

"Thank you, Violet, that will be all."

Verena stretched her arms and climbed out of her bed. Her pink silk dress was hanging up on the armoire. It was the same one that she had worn to her coming-of-age ball only a few months previously.

'I cannot face another unpleasant scene with Papa,' she told herself as she dressed, 'I must make every effort to be as compliant as he wishes.'

Entering the dining room, Verena saw that her father and her stepmother were already seated.

"I must apologise," said Verena, simply, "I am afraid my ride this afternoon quite tired me and I fell asleep. I do hope that I have not inconvenienced you with my late arrival."

"Your stepmother and I have something we wish to discuss with you, but more of that later. First, I want you to tell me how that fine stallion of mine is coming along."

Verena seized the chance to steer the conversation away from awkward matters. Her father's love of horses was one of the joys of life they had always shared.

"He is a strong-willed beast, Papa, but oh, how he runs! I feel as if I am flying when I'm mounted upon him.

He is as fearless as a lion and takes jumps as if he had wings –"

"It all sounds most dangerous to me," intervened the Countess, "my Lord, are you happy with your only daughter taking part in such pursuits? Gentle cantering is fine for a lady, but this rough and tumble is most unbecoming for an Earl's daughter. A lady never goes for jumps, she merely trots."

The Earl coughed in order to disguise a smile. He loved Verena's spirit. She was as fearless as any man when it came to horses and secretly, he was proud of her for it.

"I do not see any harm in the pursuit," he began, "I approve of healthy, outdoor activities – none of this sitting around like London ladies, getting more wan by the second!"

"Ah, I am quite in agreement with you on that count, my Lord, but it does not do for a young woman to be cavorting around the countryside like a vagabond. There is not a gentleman in London who would find that attractive."

Verena looked up from her hare soup.

"I would not care for a gentleman who did not enjoy the thrill of a cross-country gallop," she commented.

Her words dried on her lips as, for the first time, she caught sight of what her stepmother was wearing around her neck.

"Pardon my curiosity," Verena started, "but that emerald necklace you are wearing – I am sure my mother owned one very similar."

"It *was* your mother's and we will hear no more about it," snapped the Earl.

The Countess fingered the trinket hanging from her far-from-slender neck and smiled to herself.

"Jewels like this deserve to be worn, not kept locked away in a box," she remarked smugly.

Verena remained silent for the rest of the meal. She could hardly bear to look either her father or her stepmother in the face. Instead, she stared miserably into her plate, hardly touching what was placed in front of her.

"Not hungry?" asked the Countess, as the strawberry *soufflé a la Parisienne* was taken away uneaten, "I do hope you are not sickening for something? We have a very busy weekend planned for you and I want to make sure that you are looking your very best."

Verena sat silent and questioning. The tension in the air was palpable. Her father looked most uncomfortable as he cleared his throat, "Your stepmother and I –"

"What your father is trying to say," interrupted the Countess, "is that it is high time you were wed. I was shocked to hear that you went through your London Season without attracting any suitors and we both believe that twenty-one is the absolutely oldest you can be if you are to have any hope of making a good match."

Verena was speechless. The blood was draining from her head and she felt as though she might faint.

Her stepmother continued without pausing,

"I can see that there is a danger of your becoming spoiled goods if you are not taken in hand immediately. With this in mind, I have personally selected a suitable gentleman to woo you. His name is the Duke of Dalkenneth and he will be coming this weekend for the hunt and to see if you please him. He is a well-established gentleman with lands and a title and as yet no heir. His first wife died in childbirth, along with the baby and so he seeks a young wife to take her place. It is a very good match and I cannot see any obstacles, so your father and I are both expecting you to accept his suit."

Verena turned her pleading eyes to her father, who steadfastly looked away.

"Papa?" she said questioningly.

"Your stepmother is quite right. It is high time that you were married and became Mistress of your own household. He is a fine choice and will make a most suitable match. Moreover, when your stepmother has a child, she will not want the worry of an unmarried stepdaughter."

"But Papa, when I marry, I want to marry for love like you and Mama. I do not think I could bear to be with a man I did not care for."

The Earl began to tap his fingers impatiently on the dining table.

"Daughter, your stepmother has been kind enough to undertake what you yourself seemed unable to accomplish when you were in London – she has found you an acceptable suitor. You should be grateful that she has gone to so much trouble on your behalf. You will meet the Duke of Dalkenneth and if you are lucky enough to fall in love with him, no one will be more delighted than I."

15

Verena could stand it no longer. At the risk of further angering her father, she rose from the table and left hastily without saying another word.

'How could he do this? *How could he*?' she sobbed as she ran upstairs towards her bedroom. 'I thought he loved me and now I find myself doubting him.'

Rushing past a bewildered Violet, Verena bolted into her bedroom and locked the door behind her, tears streaming down her face.

'I will not marry a man I have not chosen for myself,' she cried into her pillow, 'Mama would never have wanted this for me. But it would seem my wishes do not count. Oh, dearest Mama, I wish you were here, oh, how I need you! What will become of me? Oh, what *will* become of me!'

CHAPTER TWO

As the hours ticked by, Verena slowly composed herself.

'I *must* think of something, I cannot simply resign myself to this fate.'

She tossed and turned on top of her silk eiderdown, her hair a mass of tangles, undried tears on her cheeks.

'How wretched I will be if I am forced into a marriage against my will. No, I will *not* marry a man I do not love! I only wish I could remember why the Duke's name is so familiar to me, yet I cannot recall his face – '

The past few months had been more than enough to convince of her what a life without love would hold.

She had never known her father to be so distant with her. Only occasionally did he afford her the kind of affection they had previously shared when it had been just the two of them at Rosslyn Hall.

'Since my stepmother has arrived, it is as if he has completely forgotten Mama,' Verena moaned to herself sadly and then began to cry again. 'Truly I am starved of love and it would seem that I will wait a long time before I find love at Rosslyn Hall again.'

She gazed around the room that she had occupied since leaving the nursery and at all the familiar objects within it.

As she turned to face her bedside cabinet, she noticed that Violet had been tidying up. The jumble of books that were usually strewn across the floor by her bed had been neatly stacked with her favourite, Thomas Bulfinch's *Mythology* on the top.

Verena picked up the heavy book and sighed longingly. She fingered the cover and was immediately transported to another land.

Oh, how she loved the stories of mythical Gods and Goddesses, strange beasts in foreign climes and most of all, the story of the Trojan horse!

'How I wish that someone like Paris would come and steal me away this very night. If I was a man, I could simply disappear and travel like Odysseus or Jason and his Argonauts. But what can a mere woman do? A lady cannot simply leave as and when she pleases.'

All of a sudden her mother's face floated in front of her eyes and she could hear her soft voice telling her stories of brave Florence Nightingale, who had risked all to help the men at the Scutari hospital during the terrible Crimean War.

'And her reputation did not suffer,' recalled Verena to herself. 'So it is perfectly possible that I, too, could travel alone in the world!'

Taking comfort from the memory of her mother, her gaze alighted upon a painting of Poole Harbour hanging on the wall by her dressing table.

It was a simple scene showing the ships in their dock and the high, blue sky overhead full of the promise of dreams yet to be realised.

'What would Mama have done in my place?' she whispered to herself, 'she would never have allowed herself to be forced into a loveless union. She would have run away rather than have been made to endure a living hell – '

It was as if her mother was speaking to her while she pondered her future – Verena would never have dared to think such thoughts without some form of guidance. It went against her loyal nature.

'I have no choice, I have to leave this place. I will gladly take a risk if it will bring me the kind of happiness I long for, and the unknown has to be better than a marriage I have not chosen with a man I will despise.'

She stood up, dried her tears and walked over to the painting of Poole harbour. It seemed as if those clear blue skies were calling to her!

She had always loved the sea. Her father had a yacht moored in that very harbour and before the death of her mother he had frequently taken Verena on outings.

She remembered fondly her voyage to France en route to her finishing school in Paris when she was sixteen. It had been the year after her Mama died and she had not wanted to go, but once up on deck, with the engines on the new steam ship humming under her feet and the sea breeze in her hair, she had never felt happier.

'That's it, I will go to Poole and catch a ship to France or maybe Spain or even Greece!' The idea filled her with fire and determination.

'For once, I will not be the dutiful daughter. But I have to leave before the weekend – otherwise my fate is sealed.'

For the rest of the night Verena could hardly sleep with excitement as plans for her flight formed in her mind. She conjured up all manner of situations and hopes and fears.

'But I will be brave, I must see this through,' she vowed to herself, firmly. 'Oh, Mama, guide me! I have *never* needed you more than I do now.'

*

Verena arose the next morning, exhausted but imbued with a sense of quiet purpose.

"How is my Lady this morning?" asked Violet, as she pulled back the heavy curtains and allowed the bright sunlight to stream in. It was a fine morning that hinted at warm weather ahead.

"I am well, very well," answered Verena, a secret smile on her lips.

"I hear we are to have an important guest this weekend, my Lady. We have been told to make ready for a small hunting party. It's good to see his Lordship going hunting again."

"Yes, Violet, it is," said Verena, cautiously. She realised that she had to behave as normally as possible so as not to arouse any suspicions. "Now, where is my tea?"

The maid hurriedly brought the silver tray laid with the finest bone china.

"His Lordship and her Ladyship are already downstairs, my Lady. Will you be joining them?"

"Presently. That will be all, Violet."

Some fifteen minutes later, Verena took a deep breath as she descended the central staircase. Even though her mind was still whirling from the previous evening's decision, she as composed.

Already the house was alive with the bustle of servants preparing for the weekend.

She pushed open the dining room door and was met by the expectant stares of both the Countess and her father.

"I trust you slept well and have had time to reconsider your hasty behaviour of last night?" said the Countess, spreading honey on her toast.

Verena did not reply but simply helped herself to some kedgeree from the salver.

Her stepmother continued, "I am looking forward to planning this wedding immensely –"

"But I thought that the Duke was coming here to see if I suited?" queried Verena, "He may not like me."

A cold chill spread through Verena. Her stepmother was speaking as if everything had already been arranged and that she had already been promised to the Duke.

The thought made her even more determined to go through with her plan without any delay.

"Of course he will, you are my daughter," said the Earl gruffly, "he liked you well enough on his last visit."

He returned to the business of cracking open his egg.

Verena looked at him questioningly.

"So I have indeed encountered the Duke before?"

"Dearest, surely you have not forgotten that you have met the Duke of Dalkenneth?" he continued, not looking up from his egg. "He was here the year before last to discuss some business. He was eager for hunting, but I was in no mood for it at that time."

A vision of an ill-disposed man in his forties suddenly came shudderingly to Verena. She remembered with horror

21

his mean face and tiny black eyes like withered raisins and who had grumbled a great deal about the lack of sport.

"The Duke's wife died last year," added the Countess, "and now that his period of mourning is over, he is keen to wed again. Sadly, there was no issue from his previous union and he wants children immediately. Your offspring will inherit a sizeable fortune, not to mention vast estates in Scotland. I will look forward to being a step-grandmother."

'This evening,' she thought, in desperation. 'It *has* to be this evening that I make my escape!'

Excusing herself from the table, she slipped quietly away through the house towards the stables. Running across the courtyard, she was more determined than ever – but she needed help.

As she passed Barker's living quarters, she could see that the door had been barred and that a group of workmen were inside knocking at the plaster.

'What is going on here?' she wondered.

At the other end of the barn, she encountered a very dejected Barker, dragging a sack full of belongings behind him.

"Mornin', my Lady."

"Barker, what on earth is going on? Why are there workmen in your living quarters?"

"It's her Ladyship," he began, putting down his sack. "She wants to turn that end of the barn into more stables. She's told me that I 'ave to sleep on the floor with the 'orses, my Lady."

Verena was outraged. How dare her stepmother treat such a faithful servant in this fashion!

"I shall speak to her immediately."

"No, my Lady, please don't." sighed Barker wearily. "It may only make things worse. I am old, who would take me on if she dismisses me?"

Verena looked compassionately at the old groom. He had been employed in the household for as long as she could remember and had served her mother before her marriage.

Yet she must ask him a favour that would surely put his future in jeopardy –

"Barker, do you recall a visitor some two summers ago, one the Duke of Dalkenneth?" asked Verena as casually as she could, her heart beating wildly.

She felt as if she knew what he was about to say.

Barker nodded his head in assent.

"Believe I do, my Lady. A right piece of work too, if you don't mind me sayin' so. A fine mount he had – a black stallion not unlike your Jet and he beat him and one of my stable boys! One day he tried to set about me with a whip until your mother 'appened to come by and stepped in. I will always owe her a huge debt for that."

Verena took a deep breath.

"Barker, now I have something I must ask of you but first, have I your sworn word that you will not tell a soul?"

Tears began to fill her eyes as she pleaded with the old groom.

Barker looked at her with kindness. He loved Verena as his own and would do anything for her, but what was it that drove her to take a servant into her confidence?

"My father and stepmother have promised me in marriage to that very Duke. He is coming here this weekend to view me as he would a brood mare! Barker, I cannot stay here, but I need your help."

"I don't know, my Lady. Much as I don't care for the new Countess, she could make my life very difficult if I helped you run away. I would be ruined if she were to dismiss me."

Verena took the old man's calloused hand and looked into his eyes pleadingly, her own spilling over.

"Please, Barker, my mother would not have wanted this enforced marriage for me. All I ask is that you help me escape. It would be in the dead of night, no one would find out, *please*, I beg you. You are my only hope."

After what seemed like an eternity, the old man nodded his head with a sigh.

"Right, my Lady. We had better start making plans. Now, you take yourself off and pack while I make the light carriage ready. I'll tell the others that her Ladyship wishes to go to Bournemouth to buy a new dress tomorrow so as not to make them suspicious."

"Thank you, *thank you!*" cried Verena. "I will reward you handsomely, I promise."

"No need for that, my Lady. It's what your good lady mother would have wanted."

Verena could barely contain her excitement as she strode back towards the house. The first part of her plan was now in place!

*

All that day, she kept herself busy. After Violet had brought up the clean laundry, she took down a small leather case from the top of her armoire and began to pack.

'I have to travel light as I can easily buy new clothes once I have arrived at my destination, wherever that might be. Two dresses, a cloak, some under things and a few trinkets.'

She counted them as she packed the case. She then took out a matching vanity case with a secret. Hidden inside it was a false bottom where she would secrete her diamond necklace, some other jewels and a sheaf of five pound notes – money her mother had left her when she died.

'A small black silk bag and a purse with some silver coins, a bottle of my favourite perfume and a tiny gold mirror and comb.'

Her head felt curiously light and dizzy as she went about her business.

'I cannot believe that tonight I will leave Rosslyn Hall,' she sighed, as she looked at her reflection in her dressing table mirror.

'A new life!'

For a moment, her heart became filled with sadness.

She looked at the circular picture frame that contained a portrait of her mother. It had been taken in a studio in Bournemouth, not long before she died. Verena remembered the day well –

'Mama, wherever I travel, you are coming with me! Then it will be as if you are watching over me and guiding my every move.'

Just then there came a knock on her door – it was Violet. Verena could see the door handle flailing wildly up and down. Violet could not enter as she had locked the door.

"My Lady, the Countess wishes to see you downstairs in the garden room," she called through the door.

"Tell her I am not yet dressed. I will be down in ten minutes," shouted Verena, hastily sliding her cases under the bed. "I have a slight headache."

Verena prepared herself to face her stepmother for the last time. Smoothing back her hair, she unlocked the door and walked slowly downstairs.

Verena looked up wistfully at the paintings of her ancestors on the stairway and ran her hand along the carved handrail.

So many memories! But she must be strong, there was so much at stake.

Entering the garden room, she could see her stepmother was seated, reading a sheaf of menus.

"Ah, Verena."

"You wanted to see me, stepmother?"

"Yes, there are a few items I wished to go over with you for the weekend."

"Naturally," replied Verena coolly, the very model of obedience.

"Firstly I have instructed Violet that she is to dress your hair up and to make sure if you go outdoors that you are wearing a hat at all times," declared the Countess. "I do not wish the Duke to form a bad impression of you or to think that you are beyond control. You must act and appear the perfect lady. Is that understood?"

Verena nodded eagerly.

The Countess regarded her sternly for a second.

"Secondly, you will make yourself available to the Duke whenever he is in the house. I do not wish you to go riding or hunting all weekend. You may partake of ladylike pursuits such as needlework or painting only, is that clear?"

"Utterly, stepmother."

"Good. I can see that you have come round to my way of thinking. I am pleased that you have seen sense at last."

"Stepmother, may I be excused dinner this evening? Violet can bring me a tray. I wish to retire early so as to look my best."

The Countess smiled, confident that she had won.

"Of course, my dear. I am glad that you are taking your responsibilities so seriously."

Verena turned and smiled to herself. This was a clever stroke on her part indeed. Tonight she would be free to start her new life away from Rosslyn Hall.

*

It was gone midnight when Verena arose, having only slept fitfully. She was too excited to do more than merely doze.

At the appointed hour, she slid her cases out from under the bed as silently as she could. Tiptoeing around the room, she caught up her cloak and boots and laid them across her waiting cases. Although it was nearly summer, she did not want to risk being caught in a downpour and getting wet feet.

She quickly put on a plain cotton dress as she did not want to draw attention to herself and she tied up her hair into a loose ponytail.

She waited until the house was absolutely quiet and she was sure that the last maid had gone to bed before opening her bedroom door. Turning, she looked quickly around the room for one last time.

'No going back,' she whispered to herself and closed the door behind her.

The house was more or less in darkness, save for the few gas lamps in the corridor. She hurried down to the back door and opened it slowly, hoping that the hinges would not creak and wake the scullery maid who was snoring nearby.

The moonlight shone through the glass door as she edged it open and slid outside.

Running across to the stables, she could hear the horses snuffling and blowing.

As she approached the barn door at the far end, Barker emerged clad in a cloak and hat she had never seen before.

"This way, my Lady," he hissed.

He took her to the rear of the stables where a small carriage was tethered to a single horse. The horse shook its mane and looked most displeased to be up at this hour.

"Give me your cases, my Lady!"

It was then that Verena realised that she had forgotten her handbag!

"Oh, no, I have to go back. I have left my bag behind!

With bated breath, she made her way back across the courtyard to the kitchen door and ran as quietly as she could through the house.

As she approached her room, she suddenly heard a noise behind her.

She turned to see Sarah, the Countess's maid, standing behind her, candle in hand, dressed in her nightclothes.

"My Lady?" she questioned with just a shadow of a sneer on her face. "Running away from us?"

Verena turned pale in the darkness.

Could Sarah have guessed her plan? Surely she had been careful enough? She had not told a soul apart from Barker and he would never betray her.

"Alas! You have caught me red-handed," she bluffed and then laughed. "I could not sleep for excitement anticipating this weekend, so thought that a walk around the grounds might calm me. I now find myself quite tired out, so if you will excuse me –"

Sarah regarded her for a second.

"Then I'll wish you good night, my Lady."

Verena heaved a sigh of relief as Sarah disappeared off down the corridor. She quickly retrieved her bag from her room and waited until she heard the servant mount the stairs to the attic bedrooms.

'I cannot let my nerve desert me now,' she told herself, as she hurried back along the corridor.

Barker was waiting anxiously for her by the stables.

"Thank Heavens, there you are, my Lady. I had started thinking you had changed your mind."

"I was apprehended by my step-mother's maid," explained Verena, climbing into the carriage, "now, let's be gone before anyone else wakes up."

Barker tipped his hat and walked the horse and carriage out of the stables and towards the road that wound away from the house. Rosslyn Hall had many entrances apart from the main approach and they were making their way along the route that the service carriages used when delivering goods.

"You haven't told me yet, my Lady, where we are going?"

"Poole Harbour. From there, I do not yet know."

"Surely it isn't safe for a young lady to be travelling on her own? No chaperone! The Countess would not approve."

"I have no choice, Barker, I will be safe enough. I feel as if my mother is watching over me."

"I do hope she is," sighed the old groom.

He led the horse and carriage down to the rear gates of the park. As they approached, he took out a large key, unlocked the gates and then steered his precious cargo through.

On the other side, he locked the gate behind him and pocketed the key.

"Right-o, then my Lady. Hold on tight, I 'ave to be back before dawn if I'm not to be discovered."

Verena's mind was whirling as Barker cracked the whip over the brown mare's elegant head and the carriage jerked into motion.

On and on they sped through the night, through the village without seeing another soul, over the heath and away in the direction f the coast.

'What will my father do when he discovers I have gone?' thought Verena. 'Will he send out a search party? Will he catch me before I even get on a ship?'

So many questions – it seemed as if her head was bursting. It was only the calming vision of her mother that sustained her as the carriage plunged on into the night.

Verena wrapped her cloak tightly around her. It was so dark out that she could not even make out the passing countryside. She wondered how Barker knew the way, but as he had lived in these parts for most of his life, she reckoned that he would have found the way even if he had been blindfolded.

She was close to nodding off as they approached Barbeck Bridge. The carriage rumbled over the rough cobbles and jolted her out of her slumber. As they reached the other side, the brown mare's fetlock suddenly gave way as she stumbled into a pothole.

"Woah!" shouted Barker, as he tried to steer the carriage. It was too light to be stable and was wobbling alarmingly.

"Woah! Steady. I can't control you, you silly 'orse."

The mare had bolted and was taking off aimlessly.

Verena screamed as one of the carriage wheels hit a post.

There was a sickening scraping noise as the carriage listed over to one side and came to rest in a ditch. The mare still tethered o the carriage was whinnying shrilly.

Verena had been thrown to the floor, bumping her head on the door. She felt dizzy and somewhat shaken.

Outside she could hear Barker's soothing voice as he attempted to calm the horse. She was aware that something was very wrong.

"Woah, steady on, Jessie," called Barker to the snorting horse. "Now this is a fine mess we're in."

Verena picked herself up off the carriage floor and opened the door. She gasped when she saw the wheel – it had come clean off in the collision and was lying on the ground.

"I'm afraid we've had a bit of an accident, my Lady," said Barker, tightening the mare's reins. "I'd better see if I can fix the damage we've done."

"Oh, no, this is terrible! We are sure to be discovered. I will never get away." she groaned, wringing her hands.

Verena was frantic with fear. How would they reach the harbour now?

CHAPTER THREE

"Oh, this is hopeless!" cried Verena, as she stepped out of the crashed carriage to survey the damage.

"Are you hurt, my Lady?"

Barker was standing by the side of the road, scratching his head.

"Seems like Jessie managed to sheer off some bolts when she hit that there post."

He remained there for what seemed to Verena like an eternity without speaking another word.

Finally, she could bear it no longer. Time was ticking away and for every second they waited, for all she knew, her father could be in close pursuit.

"Please, Barker, is there anything you can do? I do not wish to sound impatient, but I am afraid that my absence will be discovered."

"I just need to find something to fix this wheel back on and we'll be away in no time," he announced. "If I'm not mistaken, there's a tool bag in the luggage compartment with some odds and ends in it – I remember seeing it there when I went to load in your cases, my Lady."

"As quick as you can," urged Verena.

The old groom was soon rummaging around the luggage compartment, puffing and blowing as he tried to see in the dark.

Verena could barely contain her anxiety.

Just then, the moon peeked out from behind a bank of cloud and bathed the carriage in a brilliant glow. It was like a torch from Heaven.

"Well, thanks be to the Lord," muttered Barker, "seems like 'im upstairs has taken pity on us."

Barker suddenly gave a yelp of delight and walked towards Verena, looking very pleased with himself.

"Here it is, my Lady. Just what I need to fix that there wheel."

He was holding aloft a leather bag. Verena looked at him quizzically.

"Nuts and bolts, my Lady."

Verena heaved a sigh of relief.

"Now, if you can just give me a hand putting this carriage to rights?"

Verena stared at him in horror.

"Come now, my Lady. A few good shoves will get it back on the road. Jessie is happy enough where she is and we need to get to work while she rests. She's got some miles to cover yet awhile if we are to make the harbour before dawn."

There was nothing for it but to help Barker heave the coach back upright.

"One big shove, now, my Lady and we're there."

Verena was glad of the dark as she felt quite sure that her appearance was most unattractive at this moment.

With one last effort, the carriage slowly rolled back upright. Barker chocked up the wheel arch with stones and set to work.

"Pass me that mallet, will you, my Lady?"

Verena pulled a large wooden object out of the leather bag and handed it to Barker. Truly, this was a real adventure, even if she had not foreseen this particular turn of events.

With solid blows, Barker drove the last bolt into place and then carefully tightened the nut. He wobbled the wheel to and fro to test the fixings, before pronouncing himself satisfied.

"Aye, that will do. Let's get Jessie tethered back up and be on our way. It'll be getting light afore long."

Verena walked swiftly over to the grazing horse and grabbed hold of her bridle.

"Come on, girl. Time for you to run like the wind!"

The horse flicked its ears as if it could understand her every word.

As Barker hitched her up once more to the carriage, Verena clambered on board. She rubbed at her aching temple.

Barker cracked his whip once more over Jessie's head and the carriage took off into the night. Verena turned round to watch the bridge vanish in the distance, still convinced that she would see a party of horsemen coming after them.

But no such sight appeared.

Mile after mile they ploughed on through the gloom.

Neither Verena nor Barker spoke. It was the stuff of nightmares – the endless dark countryside speeding by – the odd snatch of moonlight poking through the clouds – strange shapes looming up in front of them out of the dark.

"How much further?" she shouted to Barker, after they had been travelling for quite some time.

"Only a few miles to go – look, you can see the sky is brighter ahead of us. It's the harbour lights."

Sure enough, Verena could see a dim, hazy glow, like the warmth from a faraway fire. Behind her, the night sky was giving way to the lavender-coloured dawn.

'We will not get there before dawn,' she muttered to herself. 'How will I go unrecognised? My father has so many friends in Poole and the Harbour Master has often dined at the Hall. What shall I say should I bump into him?'

These and a thousand other thoughts chased through her mind. With every passing mile, she became more and more anxious.

At last, they arrived in Poole.

The carriage did not slow down, but sped on through the dark, narrow streets, Jessie's hooves resounding sharply over the cobbles.

Verena could now smell salt in the air and felt the sharp breeze.

As the carriage swung into Poole harbour, she was amazed to see that it was a hive of activity.

Porters ran past balancing baskets on their head, official-looking men in uniforms bustled around waving papers. Everywhere people were doing deals and going about their business and it could not have been any more than four thirty in the morning.

"Aye, these 'arbour folk work while the rest of us are tucked up in bed," exclaimed Barker, as if he had read her thoughts. "Now, if my memory serves me well, the ticket office is just around this bend to the right."

Barker brought the carriage to a halt outside a wooden building on the quayside.

It was strangely quiet. It occurred to Barker that maybe her Ladyship was going to find difficulty in locating a ship to take her. She was, after all, travelling alone without a companion.

'This is it,' said Verena to herself. 'I cannot go back now.' She opened the carriage door and stepped out. Barker was already unloading her luggage.

How insubstantial it now looked sitting on the quayside!

"Barker, you must return to the Hall immediately," suggested Verena firmly. "No one must discover that you and the carriage are missing."

"It may be too late for that, my Lady," Barker gestured towards the lightening sky. "It will be breakfast time when I get back."

Verena fumbled inside her purse and brought out a few silver coins she had put there earlier, expressly for this purpose. She pressed them into Barker's hand.

"My Lady, I told you, there is no need –"

"Barker, I insist. Take it. That is an order."

She pressed the coins into his calloused hand.

The old man had tears in his eyes as they said their goodbyes.

"Who knows if I will ever see you again, but thank you, thank you, Barker, from the bottom of my heart. Now go!"

She watched as Barker climbed up onto the carriage and urged Jessie to walk on.

"Good luck, my Lady!" he called, as the carriage edged away from the quayside. "God bless!"

*

For the first time ever, Verena was alone, utterly alone. She walked nervously towards the ticket office. She could see a bright light burning there, but as she entered, there were few people inside.

A young man, not much older than she, sat behind the glass at the counter. He wore his hair slicked back with a thin moustache in the London fashion.

She approached the booth and waited for him to notice her presence.

"Can I help you, madam?" he enquired.

"I wish to sail to France," began Verena, her voice quivering. "When is the next sailing?"

The man clicked his tongue.

"Sorry, madam, but you've just missed the last one for a while. It's the tide you see, it's going out."

The words hit Verena like whip blows.

No more ships. This could not be true!

"When is the next one? Surely there must be another later on today?"

"Not until six o'clock this evening. Sorry, miss."

Verena walked away from the counter, thoroughly dejected. To think she had come this far to be thwarted.

Weeping silently, she sat down on a hard wooden bench in the corner.

'If I wait until the next sailing, I will surely be discovered. Oh, what can I do?' She looked around the ticket office, taking in every last detail – the polished wooden floor, the wainscoting on the walls and the cream paint. There was a notice board with sailing times and an advertisement for a yacht for sale.

She had heard her father commenting on how the new steam ships had now become so fashionable and a few of his friends were selling their old brigs with sails for one of the new-fangled craft.

Verena rose and wandered over to the notice board. Sure enough, as she ran her finger along the timetable, there was a sailing to Cherbourg at six o'clock – over twelve hours hence.

'I simply cannot wait that long. I am sure to be discovered if I have not left here soon.' It was then that her eyes alighted upon a neat, handwritten notice on creamy vellum. Her heart beat faster as she read the words, CHEF REQUIRED URGENTLY Top-class French chef for a three month period. Must be able to create authentic haute cuisine dishes, Apply The Seahorse, Poole Harbour.

Verena's mind whirled.

At her finishing school in Paris she had always come out with top marks in the *haute cuisine* class. Mademoiselle Dupont had often gone into ecstasy over her *supreme de volaille* and had declared her *madelines* almost as good as those found in the local *patisseries*.

She had spent many a happy hour at Rosslyn Hall in the kitchen, cooking tempting morsels for her father when he experienced dark days and had refused to eat.

Verena tore the notice off the board and strode up to the counter, full of confidence. The young man fingered his moustache and looked querulously at her.

"Can I help you?"

"This advertisement, can you tell me where I can find the Seahorse?"

The young man studied the leaflet she held out to him and gave a dismissive sigh.

"This here gentleman won't have women on board," he said, going back to his work.

"But I do not understand – " began Verena. "What do you mean?"

"Like I said, miss. The gentleman what owns the *Seahorse* refuses to have women on board – chef or no chef. It's men only on board that ship. He's most particular."

Verena felt utterly deflated.

'No, I cannot be defeated now I am so close. I must think, *I must think*.' Slowly a plan formed in her mind. It was daring, it was shocking, but she was desperate.

'If Joan of Arc can join the French army, then surely I can become a French chef,' she declared to herself, marching out of the ticket office. 'Now all I need is a willing accomplice to help me on my way – '

*

Poole Harbour was once one of the richest ports in the South-West of England, but in these dying years of the century, it found itself to be a poor shadow of its former self. The fishing fleet was much depleted and it was mainly commercial and passenger craft that found haven in the harbour.

The sun was up and shining brightly down on Verena as she began to walk the streets around the harbour. There were many taverns, surprisingly full and she passed them quickly, scared of the comments of the rough-looking sailors who hung around the doorways.

'I must find some suitable attire,' she muttered to herself, as she steeled her nerves. 'But where can I find someone to help me?'

She now found herself in a narrow sleepy street. She was tired and hungry. She had eaten very little the previous evening and she was feeling quite faint.

Nearby a little baker's shop was open with the delicious smell of newly baked bread wafting out of the door.

Verena entered the shop and was pleased to see a few tables and chairs set out.

Sinking gratefully down, she ordered tea and bread, butter and jam. The young waitress who served her gave her a strange look, but she ignored her and ate the thick slices with relish.

At that moment a young sailor boy came in. By this time, the shop had become quite full and the only available seat was opposite Verena. He spied it and came over.

"Scuse me, miss, is this seat taken?"

An idea was forming in Verena's mind as she shook her head and gestured for the boy to sit down.

He was no more than fifteen, slender and about her height. He wore a loose navy serge jacket and three quarter length trousers. A jaunty cap sat atop his blond curls and his eyes were as blue as the sea.

"Don't mind if I join you?" he grinned.

Verena smiled graciously. She had to be charming.

The waitress brought the boy eggs and bread.

'I must seize this opportunity,' thought Verena.

"Tell me," she said to the boy, "where is your ship and when do you sail?"

"Oh, I've just come off a long voyage," the boy replied, "been to New Zealand. They've natives there with faces painted so you'd swear they'd stepped straight out of a nightmare. They waggle their tongues at you like this –"

He stuck out his pink tongue and waggled it in Verena's direction. She pulled back in horror. The boy, seeing her discomfort, doffed his cap.

"Beggin' your pardon, miss."

Verena took a deep breath – she could delay no longer.

"You must allow me to buy you your breakfast and in return I would ask a favour of you –"

The boy gave her a strange look. He had been around the globe and had encountered many kinds of women, but this young and very beautiful lady was a turn if ever he had seen one.

"Go on."

"Your clothes, I need them."

He clasped his cap in mock horror to his breast. Verena realised that she had not expressed herself clearly. Blushing deeply, she corrected herself, "No, not the ones you have on. Do you have another set I could buy off you?"

At the mention of money, the sailor boy's eyes lit up.

"How much is it worth to you?"

Verena dived into her bag and proffered a handful of silver.

The boy's eyebrows shot up into his curls.

"Blimey, miss. That will do! Now, you stay here. Pay for breakfast and I'll meet you outside in fifteen minutes. A shilling deposit, that's all I ask."

Verena handed over the shilling, praying that the boy was honest. She judged however that he had an open face.

Verena hastily paid for both hers and the boy's food and then leaving a tuppenny tip for the waitress, left the shop and waited outside.

As long minutes ticked by, it seemed as if Verena had been standing there for half an hour at least.

She was just about to give up and walk away, feeling most cheated, when she saw the boy running towards her with a bag.

"Here," he puffed, as he approached her. "They ain't been washed and they're a bit messy."

"Never mind, they'll do," replied Verena, handing over fifteen shillings.

"Well, bye, miss," said the boy, touching his cap. "Ta for breakfast."

"No, it is you who I must thank."

She waved at the boy's departing figure as he disappeared into the maze of streets. Verena peered inside the bag and was temporarily overwhelmed by their musty odour.

Making her way back to the ticket office, she crept into the building and headed for the ladies cloakroom. The young man with the moustache was no longer sitting at the counter. In his place was an older man with neat ginger sideburns and a shiny face. He was adding up a column of figures and scarcely paid her any attention.

Verena squeezed herself and her luggage into one of the cubicles. As quick as she could, she pulled on the foul-smelling uniform of a shirt, jacket, trousers and cap.

'Now for the final touch!' she cried, leaving the cubicle and placing her vanity case on the sink stand.

She snapped open the latch and rummaged inside.

'Ah, there they are.' Fishing out a pair of dressmaking scissors, Verena pulled off the cap and took a deep breath.

With one swift movement, she cut a large hank of hair from the front, then another from the side, until at last, a huge pile of gleaming black hair sat in the sink.

She regarded her reflection in the dirty mirror over the sink stand. She could barely recognise the face that stared back at her. With her hair barely covering her ears, her small features stood out – as did the livid red mark where she had hurt herself earlier.

Such was the transformation that she could not suppress a gasp.

'I look like a boy!'

Placing the cap on top of her cropped head, she took one last look at herself before leaving the cloakroom.

Striding boldly up to the counter, she waited for the man's attention.

"Yes, young man?"

Verena was silently thrilled. She knew what she must now do. In a heavily French-accented voice, she spoke gruffly lowering her voice so as to appear as authentic as possible.

"*Pardon,* monsieur, the Monsieur who is wanting a chef?"

Verena raised her voice at the end of the sentence as she had heard the mademoiselles at finishing school do when they were attempting to speak English.

The man behind the counter appeared slightly flustered. He raised his voice and began pointing.

"You want the *Seahorse!*" he bellowed, "ask for Captain James Macdonald."

Verena could barely contain a smile. She had seen this performance so often when she was in Paris with English tourists.

"*Merci,* monsieur, er, where is the *Seahorse?*"

She spoke slowly and deliberately, as if each word was difficult for her to pronounce.

The ginger-haired man gesticulated wildly.

"Turn left, *left* at the pier and it is on the *right. Bon,* eh?"

Verena smiled again,

"*Oui, oui, bon.* It is good, no? Thank you."

She left the ticket office still smirking at the man's feeble attempt at French.

Her heart began to beat wildly as she came to the docks where many fine vessels were moored. She wondered what kind of ship the *Seahorse* might be – she walked past a mixture of brigs and small boats and then finally, she caught sight of a magnificent steamship sitting at the end of the line.

'This must be it, I feel it in my bones.' And sure enough, on its bow were the words, *THE SEAHORSE.*

'What a curious name for such a modern vessel,' she wondered, her heart hammering again as she walked up the gangway. 'I must say, I had not expected anything so new. I imagined something with sails.'

Up on deck, Verena could see that preparations were being made to leave. The crew were busy loading barrels and casks and she noticed a crate of mackerel, probably caught that very morning, their scales glinting in the sun. There were sacks of grain and she was surprised to see a hank of nutmegs sitting on top of several bunches of onions and strings of garlic.

'Most unusual for an English gentleman,' she mused. 'This man boasts a rare palate.'

It was then that she noticed a tall, grey-haired gentleman standing by the bridge. By his uniform she guessed that this must be the Captain. He was wearing a peaked cap, trimmed with white braid and he held a pocket watch in his hand.

"Get moving, men," he shouted to the bustling crew, "we set sail with the evening tide and we have all his Lordship's baggage to load on yet awhile."

"Aye, aye, Captain," came the chorused response.

Barely able to breathe with nerves, Verena approached the tall man.

"*Capitaine* James MacDonald?" she enquired, in her new rough, French-sounding voice.

The Captain spun round and regarded her closely before answering.

"Yes."

"I 'ave come about the position of chef to Monsieur?"

Once more, the Captain stared at Verena. For one awful moment, she feared that she was about to be unmasked.

"*Je suis*, Jean Armand," continued Verena, feeling distinctly uneasy at the man's taciturn behaviour. "I 'ave cooked the cuisine in many fine 'ouses. I learn in Paris and now, I wish to travel some more before I return."

Still silent, the Captain remained unmoved.

'What ails this man?' she thought, 'why does he not answer me?' Eventually, the Captain made a gesture for her to follow him

.

'I wonder where he is taking me. Oh, Heavens, I do hope that he is not taking me straight to his superior and they are about to clap me in jail and give me up to the police.'

Gradually, they descended the narrow stairs below decks. The walls and floors were all bolted steel, and their footsteps clanged as they made their way downward.

Finally, the Captain arrived at a partially glazed door that bore a sign reading '*Galley.*'

He pushed open the door and walked straight in, leaving Verena trailing in his wake.

She was about to protest at his rudeness, when she remembered that she was supposed to be a man and he was only treating her as he would a fellow crewmember.

'I will have to get used to this,' she scolded herself. 'I am no longer Lady Verena Rosslyn, but a common chef, Jean Armand. I must steel myself not to expect the kind of niceties that I have previously enjoyed.'

The Captain halted and spoke, "This is the galley."

Verena looked around her. It was not at all what she had expected. Spotless surfaces gleamed everywhere – she could see that the ship had one of latest fuel-burning stoves.

It was almost the same size as the one at Rosslyn Hall. Shiny, stainless steel pans were stacked up on shelves and there were several brace of pheasants hanging from hooks in the ceiling.

In the centre of the galley was a beech-topped table with all manner of knives and implements hanging from it.

She spied a tower of plates that even from a distance she could see was of fine bone china.

A pile of tammies sat neatly folded on a shelf next to a stack of bowls that ranged from one the size of a *dariole* mould to a huge great vessel that would hold nearly a gallon.

"This is the pantry –"

The Captain opened the door to a small cupboard, Verena stuck her head in and all manner of exotic smells wafted up and tickled her nostrils – cinnamon, pepper, a sharp tang of vinegar, the rich aromas of olive oil, coffee and yeast.

There were tins of anchovies, jars of *herbes de Provence* and a small casket of green olives, marinating in a rich concoction of coriander and lemon peel. She opened a flour bin and sniffed.

'French flour! I would know that smell anywhere.'

There were packets of buckwheat and rye, jars of honey and bunches of dried lavender, thyme and marjoram.

"His Lordship is very particular and will only eat French food," explained the Captain.

"The last chef we had was so terrible, we had to throw him off at Boulogne. His Lordship would hang me from the mizzen if I hired anyone else as bad."

"You will find my cuisine *tres bon*."

Verena could feel her nerves jangling. Not only did the owner want a chef, he wanted the best.

"Well, young lad, do you think I'm going to just take your word for it?"

Verena felt light-headed as the Captain considered his next sentence, an unnerving habit, she felt.

"So you won't mind, Jean Armand, if I put you to the test before I hire you, will you?"

Verena shook her head, her stomach in knots and her mind awhirl. She could not think of a single recipe at that moment, her mind was a complete blank.

What was the Captain going to ask her to do next? He appeared to be ruminating. Verena stood there awkwardly, uncomfortably hot, her cap irritating her scalp.

Finally, he spoke,

"*Oeufs en cocotte*. That will do. I assume you know how to make them?"

Verena stared at the man, her mind still empty of any inspiration.

"Well?"

"*Mais, bien sur*," she replied. "This I can do."

"I'll be back in fifteen minutes. You will find new-laid eggs on the side and I'll get the Steward to bring down some fresh milk for you straight away. The cocottes are on the shelf over there –"

"Fifteen minutes?" breathed Verena, her heart in her mouth.

"*Fifteen minutes!*" confirmed the Captain, shutting the door behind him.

Standing alone in the kitchen, Verena did not know which way to turn.

"I cannot fail, I must not!" she cried aloud. "My whole future depends on this dish being just right."

And with that, she removed her jacket and cap and took down a bowl from the shelf –

CHAPTER FOUR

Verena could see by the clock on the wall that time was ticking away.

'Now, if I can just remember Mademoiselle's secret ingredient, I can begin.'

Her thoughts were interrupted by the arrival of the Steward, carrying a large pitcher of milk covered with a cloth.

"Welcome on board," he said, "my name is Arthur. I will return later to show you to your cabin, should the Captain deem you worthy of hiring."

Verena stared after the man as he left as quickly as he had arrived.

She opened the pantry door and began to look for what she needed.

'Butter, yes, I will need some or perhaps there is some cream somewhere instead? Ah, yes, here it is.'

Her eyes then alighted upon a jar of nutmeg, some had been grated, others were intact.

'At last, Mademoiselle's secret!' she enthused, picking up the jar. 'Now, I must find the cocotte dishes.'

Climbing onto a stool that she found tucked under a counter, she searched the shelves. Eventually, she found a pile of baking tins and there, sitting on top, were four cocottes.

Carefully greasing two with butter, she placed a dessertspoonful of cream in each one, followed by a pinch of nutmeg and one of salt and pepper.

'That should enliven the dish. Now, where is the cooked ham, I am certain that I saw a leg hanging up somewhere.'

She located a ham hanging hidden behind a brace of pheasants and carved off small slithers. She then set a pan of water on to boil.

Verena anxiously glanced up at the clock – only ten more minutes. Thankfully, this dish was one of the quickest ones that a chef could make. However, although it was simple, it required a delicate touch. The version she was making was not strictly classic *oeufs en cocotte*, but she felt sure that the Captain would appreciate it nevertheless.

Gently breaking a new-laid egg into each cocotte, she placed them in the pan of boiling water and turned down the heat.

By now beads of sweat were starting to trickle down her forehead and the bump on her head was stinging.

She peeped into the saucepan and added a pinch of cayenne to the yolks.

'Almost done.'

At that moment, she could hear the heavy footsteps of the Captain returning.

'I must stay calm at all costs. I must not fail at this late stage.'

"Right, young sir. Your time is up."

"One moment, *s'il vous plait*," replied Verena gruffly.

She turned off the pan of water, carefully took out the cocottes and gingerly ran a palette knife around the inside of each one.

The eggs popped out with ease.

Verena next took down a fine bone china plate and placed the eggs in the centre, before sprinkling the finely carved slithers of ham over the top.

"*Et voila!*" she declared with a flourish.

The Captain stared at the eggs for a short while then took a fork and prodded them. He sniffed them, cut one in half and then in half again.

'Oh, do hurry up!' fussed Verena to herself. 'I cannot bear this wait. What is wrong with the man? Why can he not simply cut it and eat it.'

But the Captain was taking his time. He lifted a morsel to his mouth, allowing the thick, yellow yolk to burst and spill over his bottom lip.

"Well?"

He did not reply but cut another piece of egg and conveyed it to his mouth.

'For pity's sake. This is worse than the wheel coming off the carriage.' At last, he deigned to speak.

"Hmm, not bad," he pronounced curtly. "They're passable."

Passable! Verena wanted to beat him with her fists after the immense effort she had put into the dish. She composed herself, showing not one flicker of emotion on her young face.

"So, I am 'ired?" she asked.

The Captain put down his fork and once again wiped his mouth.

"You'll do. Now listen carefully to me, it is most important that you understand."

Verena nodded.

"You will be cooking for the Marquis of Hilchester – a most particular gentleman. He expects the highest possible standards when it comes to his food and demands the best. I think you will agree that you have a challenge ahead.

"Now, I will go and inform him of your appointment. He will be most pleased that we finally have a new chef on board. You will also be cooking for the Steward and myself, so all meals must be for three persons. You will eat with the rest of the crew. There is a cook who will be arriving shortly for this purpose. He is aware that he cannot prepare meals until you have made his Lordship's. Is that all clear?"

"*Mais, oui*, monsieur."

"Good. I might add that his Lordship speaks fluent French, so there should be no misunderstandings about his requirements. I would suggest that you plan some menus before we leave and go ashore to buy supplies. You will find some money in that tin by the stove – you will be expected to account for every last penny you spend and any deficit will be taken out of your wages."

He walked through the galley door, leaving Verena with the half-eaten plate of eggs.

'At last I am on my way,' she encouraged herself as she cleared up the dishes and began to stack them in the sink.

She looked around the galley once more. This would be her home for the next few months. She could hardly contain her excitement.

Having washed the pan and dishes, she took down the large volume marked '*Menus*' from the shelf and began to read it.

'Hmm, I can see that his Lordship does indeed have a most fine palate,' thought Verena, as she perused the bill of preferred fare.

Quickly she made a list of provisions she would need, but was interrupted when Arthur the Steward returned carrying the crate of mackerel she had seen earlier.

"You can have these to be going on with and then one of the crew will bring the rest down for you. Now, I shall show you to your cabin."

They proceeded along many long corridors until finally they reached a row of slender doors, barely the width of a fully grown adult. He opened a door near the end of the corridor and beckoned to Verena.

The cabin was very modest – a bunk, a cabinet and a small sink. The rough-looking blanket on the bed was somewhat stained and Verena shuddered at the thought of having to lie there. It was definitely not what she was used to but she would have to endure it.

"No time to waste," said Arthur, "leave your things here and you'd best be off to the market before they close. His Lordship likes everything fresh. Now I must leave you. I have to go and find the new cabin boy – he was due here three hours ago and has yet to arrive."

Verena glumly dropped her cases onto the bed and found her way slowly back to the galley.

'I will surely get lost in this maze,' she thought as she found herself in a strange part of the ship.

Eventually, Verena entered a corridor that seemed familiar and very soon she was back in the galley.

She took the tin that contained the money for supplies from the shelf and counted out four half-crowns and some coppers. Her list of what she needed lay on the beech-topped cabinet. She scrutinised it once more.

There was a wicker basket tucked under a counter near the door, so Verena took it and slipped her list inside her jacket pocket.

As she emerged blinking into the strong sunlight, she inhaled the salty air and felt excited once more.

She was on her way. *Really* on her way.

Verena quickly found the place where the fishing boats were docking and bought a fine pair of lobsters, still blue and squirming.

In spite of her being dressed as a boy, she was worried that the passing crowds would see through her disguise. But she garnered not one curious look.

"Ah, peaches. I do not believe it!" she cried in her new voice, as she spied crates of them on the quayside.

The old man who was unloading them hardly looked at her.

"Sixpence a pound to you, sonny."

Verena looked aghast. So costly. The man caught her look.

"They're from Italy and these 'ere are destined for Fortnum and Mason's. Finest money can buy."

She hesitated for a moment and then recalled the Steward's words – the Marquis liked his produce fresh. Tonight's pudding was to be one of her father's favourites – *peches a l'Australienne.*

"I will take two pounds, monsieur, but please make sure they are ripe."

The old man gathered a quantity of fruit into a small sack and handed it to Verena.

Handing over one of her half-crowns, she patiently waited whilst he dug into his pockets and brought out a shiny shilling and a sixpence.

Thrilled at purchasing the peaches, Verena ran hither and thither, ticking off her list.

'Vanilla pods straight from Madagascar, almonds from Spain, powdered carmine and a few strands of saffron –"

They all tumbled into Verena's basket.

'Now I just need some more fresh cream and I am almost done.' As she walked back through the harbour, she spied a butcher's shop. Inside the window display was a fine crown of lamb.

'Perfect for tomorrow's dinner,' she decided.

*

The afternoon sun had started to dip down into the sky by the time Verena returned to the *Seahorse*, tired yet exhilarated.

It was with a sense of sadness and feeling a little homesick that she mounted the gangway to the ship. She fervently wished that she had a companion to talk to.

'But perhaps I will find one soon enough. This other cook may be a like-minded fellow.'

Verena's basket was very heavy and being unfamiliar with the ship, she lost her footing at the top of the gangway. She struggled to keep hold of her basket and promptly dropped it.

She was aware of a howl of pain as the basket landed squarely on the toes of the distinguished gentleman who was standing on the deck.

"Oh, *pardon*, monsieur," she muttered quickly, gathering up the basket and a few loose peaches that had slipped out of the sack.

Without waiting or looking to see whom she had injured, Verena ran quickly below.

Her heart beat wildly. She crouched on the stairway as she heard the Captain rush over to the gentleman on deck.

"Your Lordship," he was saying, "are you hurt? Did you see who was responsible for this?"

Verena heard a deep manly voice replying,

"It was only a boy, Captain. I did not see his face. The fellow was wise enough to make himself scarce."

"It must be the new cabin boy, your Lordship. I will have him soundly thrashed for his carelessness as soon as I find him."

'Oh no,' gasped Verena, still hiding on the stair. 'That must have been the Marquis of Hilchester! I cannot allow the new cabin boy to take the blame for me. I must confess at once.'

She heard a slight commotion above and then the Marquis's deep tones moving off down the port side of the ship. Verena waited until she judged he was a sufficient distance away and then she bolted back up the stairs and out onto the deck.

The Captain was heading for the bridge.

"Wait, *Capitaine*, wait."

"Ah, Jean, I trust you are settling in?"

"Yes, *Capitaine*, but there is something I 'ave to tell you."

There was an agonising silence as the taciturn Captain waited for Verena to speak.

"It was not the cabin boy who 'urt 'is Lordship, it was *moi*. Please, do not beat the boy, you may punish me instead."

Captain MacDonald regarded Verena's worried face with amusement for some moments and then spoke,

"Be off with you, my boy. I am not about to tan the hide off the new chef – you might put hot peppers in my dinner tonight. Now mind you keep out of his Lordship's way in future. He likes his staff to be seen and not heard."

He walked off laughing, leaving Verena red-faced with indignation.

'Well. What a rude man! I've a good mind to put prunes in his pudding. This Marquis sounds a most unpleasant fellow, I do hope that I have not flown from one awful situation into another.'

It took her some time to find the galley but when she pushed open the door, she found a short, dark man inside. He was wearing a white cap and a large, striped pinafore.

"Ah, you must be the new chef," he said smiling. "My name is Jack, I'm the cook for all us 'ere serfs!"

Verena managed to force a smile, the man was so rough and ready – he looked as if he was far too dirty to be in charge of food.

"I am Jean," she responded simply.

"French, eh?" declared the man, squinting hard at her.

"*Oui,*"

"Hmm, so was the last one and a right parcel of trouble he was. You keep out of my way and I'll keep out yours."

His brusque manner quite took her aback. She could see that she was not going to find a confidant in Jack.

Verena carefully unpacked her goods, making sure that she kept back the bruised peaches to puree. She put the lobsters in a bucket of water and placed the crown of lamb on the lowest shelf in the pantry.

She looked again at the evening's menu.

To start – a *potage de legumes*, for the main course homard a la Milanaise and for pudding, her special peches a l'Australienne.

Just then, Arthur arrived carrying a tray of cups and saucers with a fine silver coffee pot.

"Here, his Lordship has finished with these. He's expecting his dinner at half past eight sharp. Mind you don't keep him waiting – he gets very cross when he's hungry."

"*Mon Dieu!* What kind of man is zis I work for?"

"A very fine gentleman," answered Arthur stiffly.

"I am sorry, I did not mean to be *impoli*."

There was a tense atmosphere for a moment.

'Oh, I have offended the Steward,' thought Verena, 'this will not do, I need him as an ally.' "Please, take this peach, it is, 'ow you say, 'urt?"

She held out one of the bruised peaches to Arthur, who regarded it closely before taking it.

"Thank you, young man. Did you say your name was Jean?"

Verena nodded.

"Well, you look after me, Jean, and I will keep an eye out for you. That's the way we do it on board the *Seahorse*, isn't that right, Jack?"

"Ar," growled the cook, chopping a side of fatty pork into strips.

"Tell me, do you know where we are going?" asked Verena hopefully.

Arthur shrugged.

"Wherever his Lordship fancies. It may be Africa, it may be India, who knows. This voyage is only three weeks – but we go wherever the whim takes him. He's a proper gypsy is our Marquis."

Verena was quite horrified at the disrespectful way the man spoke. It made her wonder if her servants had passed such judgements on her in the past.

"Now, I'll leave you to prepare the meal. Mind you do it right, Jean. We will be stopping over at one of the Spanish ports and you don't want to be set ashore in one of those stinkpots! Ha ha!"

He left the galley chewing on the peach.

61

Verena began to prepare the meal.

She winced as she threw the live lobsters into a pot of boiling fish stock and white wine – their screams resounded around the galley, while Jack laughed callously. "Ah, that will teach 'em," he chuckled.

Poor Verena always hated this part of cooking, but her father's cook had always told her that it was steam escaping from their shells, not the cries of the lobster that made such a sound.

Once they had turned pink, she fished them out of the pot and left them to keep warm between two plates over the boiling liquid. The sauce was a most complicated one – it had to perfectly complement the subtle flavour of the lobsters.

She pureed the tomatoes and added Italian hard cheese and some of the cream she had bought that very afternoon.

She was aware of Jack scrutinising her every move. He watched her with the keen eyes of a hawk.

*

At eight o'clock, the Steward returned to take up the plates and the buffet trays.

He had just picked up a pile of china from the stack, when there was a tremendous roaring noise from beneath their feet.

"*Alors*! What is zat!" exclaimed Verena, only just remembering in time to use her French voice.

"It's the ship's engines," replied Arthur.

"So we are on our way!"

Verena was breathless with nerves, the meal was almost ready, but would it be good enough for the fastidious Marquis?

As the ship pulled out of Poole Harbour she found herself beset by anxiety.

Would she be able to attain the high standard demanded by the Marquis, or would she find herself stranded in some unfriendly Spanish port? She shuddered as she bustled around the galley – her fate in the lap of the Gods.

CHAPTER FIVE

The tension in the galley was unbearable.

As precious minutes ticked away bringing her deadline of half past eight ever nearer, Verena suddenly became clumsy.

She dropped the soup ladle with a resounding crash on the floor and then spilt hot soup on her hand as she attempted to pour it into the bone china tureen.

Jack the cook sat back and chuckled, sucking on a pencil.

"Why, I ain't making you nervous, young lad, am I?" he taunted.

Verena forced a smile and pushed a lock of stray hair from her forehead. She picked up a dishcloth from the sink and began to wipe up the spilled soup.

Jack pointed the pencil in the direction of Verena's temple, where she had pushed away the lock of hair to reveal the red wound sustained in the accident with the carriage.

"That's quite some knock you've had to your head, boy. How did you get that?"

"Oh, it's nothing. I banged ze 'ead, zat's all," she mumbled.

The rough cook chuckled to himself once more and shifted in his seat.

"More like got into a fight over some bit of petticoat!"

Verena was forced to hide her shock at the man's coarse way of speaking.

The door opened and Arthur appeared wearing a clean uniform. He had brilliantine on his hair and had washed his face and shaved. He entered buttoning up his white gloves as he pushed open the galley door.

"Ready, Jean? Mustn't keep his Lordship waiting."

Verena sprinkled the last few fragments of parsley over the top of the soup and handed the tureen to him.

He loaded the tureen onto the dumb waiter near the door and caught up a sheaf of napkins.

Verena heaved a sigh as she pulled on the ropes of the dumb waiter. The tureen slid out of sight –

"Now for the *homard*," she announced,

She poured the *Milanaise* sauce into a *bain marie* of boiling water and waited for it to heat up. While it was coming to a simmer, she artistically arranged the lobsters on a large salver.

By the time the sauce was nice and hot, Arthur was back in the galley, waiting for the next course.

"Ready?"

Verena nodded her head.

Arthur carefully placed the lobsters onto the shelf of the dumb waiter while Verena brought out the cold cuts and a dish of sautéed potatoes.

"I'll take these upstairs myself," said Arthur, "and then I'll send the remains of the first course back down the chute."

The remains! Verena was sick with anticipation.

"I 'ope that there are none," she said.

There had been no word from the Marquis as to whether or not the soup had pleased him and if the dishes came back down full, she would know the awful truth.

There was an agonising wait before there was a pull on the ropes of the dumb waiter and the tureen appeared. A soup plate was balanced alongside.

Verena could scarcely bear to look as she pulled the tureen off the shelf first, followed by – an empty soup plate!

"Don't get too excited, his Lordship might have thrown it to the fishes," cackled Jack.

Verena glared at him but did not reply.

'I fear I will have to ignore this dreadful man,' she mused, 'I must not let him undermine me. I am good cook. If he is so wonderful, why has he not been offered the position of chef?'

Gingerly, she took the lid off the tureen. It was difficult to tell how much soup the Marquis had consumed. It looked to her as if it had been barely touched.

'I will not let this disturb my concentration,' she resolved, pushing the tureen to one side. 'I will make the pudding one that the Marquis will never forget.'

She had chosen an exquisite Venetian glass dish on which to present the peaches. She had found it tucked away in the pantry whilst looking for castor sugar.

She piled up the fruit that had been carefully stuffed with almond paste and then glazed with sugar and maraschino cherries. As a finishing touch, she placed some sprigs of mint around the edge of the dish and added a light dusting of icing sugar.

"*Voila!*" she exclaimed proudly.

The Steward reappeared and took a step back as he caught sight of the elegant dish of peaches.

"Well, now there's a sight. A real bobby-dazzler! Let's see what his Lordship makes of these."

He lifted the glass dish from the table and disappeared back upstairs.

The grinding of the dumb waiter announced the return of the main course. Verena's heart was beating hard as the crockery arrived.

"But these are plates that have not been used," she cried in dismay, unloading the untouched china.

"Bad luck, my lad," cackled Jack. "Better get ready to pack your things up."

Verena had to compose herself.

'I will not cry,' she told herself, 'I must not. To do so would be to attract suspicion and unwanted attention. No man would shed tears over such a trifle.'

The opening of the galley door announced the arrival of the Steward. He coughed and then beckoned to Verena.

"What is it, monsieur?" she asked, nervously.

"It's his Lordship, he requests your presence upstairs in the Saloon."

"I'll wager someone is getting off at Cadiz," gloated Jack with glee, "such a short acquaintance!"

Verena looked aghast at her flour-covered apron and pushed a damp lock of hair out of her eyes.

"Impossible," she declared, "I cannot see 'is Lordship like this."

She gestured to her apron and her face. Sweat was stinging her wound and her cap was once more irritating her immensely.

"His Lordship hasn't asked you upstairs to inspect your uniform," said Arthur, not taking no for an answer. "He isn't used to being refused. Now, if you please, Jean, you will accompany me."

Both Verena and Arthur stood for some moments, each waiting for the other to make the first move. Finally, Verena relented.

She took off the dirty apron and wiped her face on a towel. She checked that her hands were clean and then followed him out of the galley door.

She could hear Jack laughing out loud behind her as she mounted the stairs to the main living quarters.

"But the dinner, did 'is Lordship find it to 'is liking?"

Verena tugged at Arthur's sleeve but he simply shrugged.

"I am sure you will find out presently," was all he would say.

The ship was gently swaying as they emerged up on deck. She grabbed the rail as the ship suddenly pitched to one side as Arthur laughed, "You'll soon find your sea legs, young man!"

Even though the sea was not that rough, the swell was sufficient to make the ship lurch every now and then as they hit a current.

"It is always like this in the Channel," he explained, "you'll find we will be an even keel once we've hit the Bay of Biscay."

Verena began to feel quite ill and she was not sure if it was the pitching of the ship or whether it was nerves. She had never been seasick before.

The Saloon was to the rear of the bridge of the ship. Its etched glass windows sparkled with light from the candles within. Verena thought the effect most charming.

Arthur walked up to a pair of ornate double doors, knocked and waited.

"Enter," came the deep velvety tones of the Marquis.

'I shall know my fate soon enough,' thought Verena, following the Steward into the Saloon. 'Oh, I do hope he will be kind to me.'

The Marquis of Hilchester was seated at the head of a small walnut table, his intent gaze focused on the glass of fine ruby port in front of him.

Verena almost gasped aloud when she caught sight of him. Far from being the rather stately and aged gentleman of her imagination, the Marquis of Hilchester was a good-looking young man, no older than thirty-five.

'So handsome,' she sighed to herself, 'and so young.'

She noticed that his dark hair was thick and wavy and beneath strong brows were eyes of the most startling shade of liquid amber she had ever seen. She tried not to stare rudely so averted her gaze.

The Saloon was full of rare and wonderful objects and the furnishings were of the highest quality. Verena knew immediately that money had been no object when furbishing this particular room – from the fine, mahogany panelling on the walls to the Waterford crystal decanter in front of the Marquis, everything was the best available and all in the most exquisite taste.

"My Lord, this is Jean, the new chef."

Verena was captivated by her surroundings and could barely utter a word.

She looked nervously around the room, marvelling all the while at the contents. She sensed that the Marquis's eyes were upon her, taking in every detail.

"Jean, may I compliment you on a most fine meal," began the Marquis, averting his eyes as he spoke, "the peaches were especially delicious. I trust that I can expect tomorrow's fare to be of an equally high standard?"

He paused and looked at a point somewhere off into the distance.

Verena, however, was too lost in the beauty of the room and did not see him look away. Her attention had been caught by a complete, gold-tooled, leather-bound set of *"The Legends of Ancient Greece"* upon a bookshelf, just to the right of the Marquis.

"Jean, his Lordship is addressing you."

Arthur spoke brusquely and Verena immediately felt shy and unsure of herself.

'I cannot meet the Marquis's eyes,' she said to herself, 'I cannot.' "Jean?" repeated Arthur, impatiently.

"Ah, *oui*, thank you, my Lord. I can promise you zat."

With her heart hammering in her bosom, Verena looked up for the first time at the Marquis. To her surprise, she found that he would still not look her in the eye. Instead, he continued to stare into the distance, as if to search for some sign of land.

Verena felt the blood rising in her cheeks, once again forgetting her lowly station.

'How rude not to meet my gaze. Is he shy or is so full of arrogance that he deems a servant unworthy of his full attention?'

The Marquis resumed speaking,

"Your cuisine has a familiar flavour to it, the lightness of touch, the garnishes so particular – tell me, have I eaten your food before now? Maybe at the Duc du Chambercy's chateau?"

"No, my Lord. I do not know this Duc," replied Verena blushing deeply.

"Arthur tells me that you trained in Paris. Tell me, under whose tutelage did you study? I know many fine chefs in that city."

'But not Mademoiselle Dupont of the *Lycee des Jeunes Filles*, I'll warrant,' thought Verena.

She was starting to feel quite uncomfortable. This Marquis knew too many people. Surely it was only a matter of time before he guessed that she was not whom she said she was and she would be thrown off the ship?

"I studied with a retired chef in Orly," Verena stammered, at last. He 'ad cooked for many fine gentlemen."

"Well, he is to be congratulated on mentoring such a fine pupil," the Marquis commented. "And you were brought up in Paris, yourself?"

Verena sensed a trap. Perhaps he was trying to trick her.

'I must be careful how I answer,' she thought.

"I was born in the country, my Lord, but I went to Paris as a small child. My mother, she is from Marseilles."

"Aha," nodded the Marquis looking steadfastly into his port with the air of a man who had suddenly made a discovery. "That would explain your accent. Do you know, I could not place it until you mentioned that your mother was from Marseilles. It all makes sense now –"

Verena was almost swooning. She had managed to keep her wits about her and had overcome the first hurdle.

She waited expectantly for the Marquis to dismiss her, but he sat there stiffly, regarding the empty plate in front of him.

She glanced across at Arthur, who signalled with a slight incline of his head for her to remain where she was.

"Now, Jean, I am rather partial to seafood and as we are bound for the Mediterranean, I shall expect many new delicacies brought to my table to delight my palate," pronounced the Marquis. "I have a fancy for some octopus. You do know how to prepare and cook octopus, I assume?"

Verena stared at him in mute horror. Octopus! She had not even realised that one could eat it.

"Ah, I see you do not understand the English word? Let me see – in French it is *le poulpe. Alors, vous comprenez?*"

The Marquis spoke with hardly a trace of an English accent as he continued in French for some minutes.

'Thank Heavens I am fluent,' thought Verena, as she replied to the Marquis's excellent French. 'My year at finishing school was not a waste of time at all. Quite the opposite. Without the knowledge I gathered there, I would surely have come adrift. I'd like to kiss Mademoiselle Dupont, God bless her!'

The Marquis arose and the Steward swiftly moved to his aid, pulling back the elegant, balloon-back chair with its rich velvet seat.

Turning away from Verena, he strode over to a compact humidor and unlocked it. Inside were a dozen or so thick Havana cigars. Verena recognised the make – her father had preferred to smoke the very same ones. It made her feel so homesick to see their red and gold seals.

The Marquis weighed a specimen between his fingers and then sniffed it. With one swift movement, he clipped the end off and waited expectantly.

Without hesitation the Steward appeared with a lighted match.

'How elegantly he smokes,' admired Verena, her heart pounding strangely. 'He has such a noble bearing, such breeding.' The Marquis continued to peer through the windows, even though it was quite dark outside and the only signs of life were the lanterns on deck.

"I should tell you that we are on our way to Gibraltar – that will be our first stop," he informed her. "You will be at liberty to go ashore and buy whatever provisions you deem necessary. Furthermore, I will expect you to purchase and prepare some of the local delicacies."

"*Le poulpe?*" asked Verena nervously. She was still wondering what on earth she would do with it should she locate some.

"Yes, and more besides, I become bored so easily," added the Marquis, still looking out to sea. He then reverted back to speaking in English.

"We will be picking up a rather special friend of mine in Gibraltar, so you should be aware that there will be one more for luncheon and dinner every evening. Now, that will be all.

Thank you, Jean and thank you, Arthur. I will not be requiring coffee this evening, so you may go."

Verena felt as if her feet had taken root. She did not want to leave the fine Saloon. She was agog at seeing the books and the hangings, the ancient artefacts and the highly polished furniture.

Arthur coughed meaningfully and Verena bowed.

"*Merci*, my Lord," she whispered.

Leaving the Saloon, she was overwhelmed with the most curious emotion.

'I feel as if I have left a part of me in that room. How can that be? What does this all mean?'

She had a strange yearning in her heart and for some reason, she felt slightly alarmed at the prospect of there being a new guest onboard in the coming days.

Verena did not go straight down below with Arthur. Instead, she paced the deck looking up at the stars.

As she stood musing, her thoughts were interrupted by the strains of a Chopin piano etude, the notes wafting on the night air.

'How curious, I do not recall seeing a piano in the Saloon. I must go and investigate.' Softly, she tiptoed along the deck until she arrived at one of the Saloon windows. She peeked in between the etching on the glass into the interior.

It was half-dark inside with only a few candles burning. The Marquis was standing over a piece of furniture that was topped with a large brass horn. She could see that he was lost in the music as he swayed gently from side to side.

'Why, it is a gramophone,' whispered Verena, 'we have one almost identical in the house in Hertford Street.' The music stopped.

Verena held her breath, what would the Marquis play next? It was so pleasant to hear music – there had been precious little around Rosslyn Hall the past few months and Verena loved it. After her mother had died, the house had been silent, but when, as her father returned to life once more, he had installed a new gramophone in Hertford Street and had bought a pile of shellac discs to play on it.

She waited eagerly by the rail of the ship, hoping that the Marquis had another disc to play.

Sure enough, the opening notes of a rather sombre tune wafted out of the Saloon. She recognised it immediately, each note resonating in her very soul.

'Oh! It's Mama's favourite piece.' The poignant strains of Beethoven's '*Pathetique*' carried her away on a wave of emotion mingled with nostalgia.

She recalled sitting at her mother's feet whilst she had played that very piece and the warmth of her against her cheek. The odour of the lavender bags that hung in the wardrobe along with her mother's clothes had comforted her and now Verena could almost smell that scent as the music swelled majestically to a climax.

Tears spilled from her eyes.

There was not a day when she did not miss her mother, but now without a friend to call her own, she missed her even more.

'I cannot stay on deck,' she said to herself, choking on her tears. 'I must go back to my cabin. If I stay here, I risk

being discovered. And I cannot let anyone see me like this.'
Verena crept along the deck towards the stairs.

*

As the ship's engines purred on into the night, she lay back on the hard bunk in utter misery.

In the hour since she had returned below, she had sobbed her heart out whilst looking at the photograph of her mother.

'I am so alone. So alone,' she cried, the rough blanket scratching her face and hands. I do not know if I can last the journey, it is too hard – '

Eventually, there were no more tears left to cry. She lay back on the hard bunk and looked out of the small porthole. Through it, she could just about glimpse one or two stars shining dimly.

She forced her thoughts elsewhere and was surprised that she returned to the events of the evening and her first meeting with the Marquis of Hilchester.

Such a fine, handsome gentleman.

Verena had met many gentlemen during her coming-out season. There had been lavish balls and much dancing. Most of her friends had filled their dance cards eagerly, flirting coquettishly with the young men, playing them off against each other.

But Verena had no such feminine wiles. She was innocently bereft of the kind of womanly tricks that others employed to ensnare unsuspecting suitors.

Her aunt, Lady Armstrong, had despaired over her lack of gentlemen callers.

"I simply cannot fathom why you do not seem to have any admirers," she had said, "you are beautiful and charming, you adore hunting and riding and you are the most perfect hostess."

"Perhaps it is because I do not seek to attract their advances," Verena had replied, demurely. "I find the whole idea of love quite frivolous."

Yet here she was, on board a strange ship heading for Heaven only knew where with her heart filled with strange longings.

Over and over she recalled the conversation she had had with the Marquis. She went over every detail of how he held his head and the tone of voice he had used.

Unable to sleep, she rose from her bunk. Standing on top of it, she could just about see out of the porthole at the stars wheeling overhead.

She was lost in a reverie dreaming of the Marquis.

A sudden chill caught her heart as she remembered his words – the special visitor, who might it be?

"It cannot be a sweetheart, surely?" she said out loud.

A grim panic overcame her. She felt short of breath.

'Why am I feeling like this? Why should it matter to me who the Marquis invites onboard? It is no business of mine.' But her heart ached strangely nonetheless.

'I will not give the matter another thought. I am being quite, quite foolish.' She lay down once more on the bunk.

But try as she might, she could not silence the beating of her heart or the strange quickening of her blood –

CHAPTER SIX

The next day Verena was woken by a series of loud bells that marked the end of the last watch. She stretched her arms up to the ceiling and felt quite tired – the night had not afforded her much rest as her mind had been so occupied.

She got up, splashed her face with water and hurriedly put on the uniform that had been left for her. She welcomed the opportunity to leave behind the foul-smelling kit that she had bought in Poole.

'I will find some Sunlight soap and give it a good scrub later,' she thought, as she pulled on the clean navy serge trousers and enveloping white overall. A white cap was the finishing touch.

She examined her face in the small mirror she had brought with her, wincing as she touched the now purple bruise on her temple.

But there was no time for vanity. The Marquis would not wait for his breakfast.

'And I want him to have the very best breakfast he has ever tasted.' Yawning, she pushed open the heavy door, to find that Arthur was already inside in his shirtsleeves polishing the silver.

"Good morning, Jean. Or should I say *bon matin*?"

"It is *bonjour*," corrected Verena, "now, I must find the rice. 'Ave you seen it?"

Arthur pointed a soupspoon over Verena's head at a high shelf.

"All grains and dried legumes are up there, I think you'll find."

"*Merci*, Ar-toor," she replied, mispronouncing his name.

"It's Ar-thur," he answered, gently teasing her.

Verena smiled, she liked Arthur. Whilst there was no doubt that he could be over-officious and just a little starchy, it was good to have a friendly face around. Especially as Jack was a most unpleasant fellow.

Verena stood on a stool and reached for the rice, but as she opened it, she noticed that the packet was full of weevils.

"Oh, *mon Dieu!*" she screamed, dropping the packet on the floor.

"Creepy crawlies?" asked Arthur. "Don't go upsetting yourself. I will fetch some more from the hold."

"But I must make his Lordship the kedgeree!" cried Verena, putting on what she hoped was a suitable tantrum. She had once seen a visiting chef to the Hall fly off into a rage simply because cook did not have the right flour for a sauce he was making.

"Don't lose your hat, I will return in a flash." Arthur put down the knife he was polishing and left the galley.

Verena was once more alone with her thoughts.

She began to flake the smoked haddock and then set a pan on the stove.

'Cream for the Marquis and butter, I think,' she smiled to herself secretly as she stirred the mixture.

'Ah, the Marquis. Why does he intrigue me so?' wondered Verena. 'He is just a man, yet he is so unlike the ones I have met before. He has such an air of mystery about him!'

She was just popping four eggs into a pan of boiling water when Arthur reappeared carrying a stack of packets.

"Rice, barley and macaroni and we will need to buy some more when we dock in Gibraltar. I'll bet you there will be nothing but that unpleasant African stuff available that they all eat instead of rice. Tastes like bird seed."

Verena took the rice and added it to another pan of boiling water and although it was only half past seven in the morning, already it was feeling more than a trifle warm.

Carefully she drained the eggs before pouring the hot creamy sauce over the haddock and the rice.

"I shall look forward to filling my stomach with that," declared Arthur, "I am rather partial to kedgeree, mind you make enough for us all now. The Captain likes it too."

"*Bien sur,*" replied Verena, handing the steaming serving dish to him, "now, this must go straight upstairs."

Arthur placed the dish on the dumb waiter and pulled the ropes.

"I will be returning after breakfast," he said, "and the Marquis may well want to discuss his requirements for luncheon with you."

"You will ask him zis?" enquired Verena, eager to see the Marquis again.

After Arthur had departed she sat and waited patiently to be summoned above deck. But breakfast came and went and the Marquis did not request her presence in the Saloon.

She felt heavy of heart as she cleared away the breakfast dishes. The Steward and the Captain were in the crew room eagerly helping themselves to kedgeree and toast.

Verena felt no hunger herself, so she took off her apron and, in spite of being warned to keep out of sight of the Marquis, climbed up on deck.

'What harm can it do? I will stay as quiet as a mouse.' The day was indeed a fine one, the sun shone brilliantly overhead and the breeze was warm and inviting.

A group of crewmen were going about their duties nearby and she could see them with their heads together talking. She edged closer so that she might hear what they were saying.

'I must find out where we are bound, I'll wager that the Captain and crew have been instructed of our movements, it is just us servants who are not privileged with that information.'

She crouched down beside a lifeboat and strained her ears. She could just about make out the thread of conversation above the screech of seagulls.

"Ar, it's Gibraltar we be docking in first, then on to Alicante,' said one.

"You don't know for certain that we'll be stopping at Alicante, I heard that it was Tangier." replied another.

"You are both wrong, it's Africa we are bound for!"

A good-natured quarrel broke out amongst the three men, amidst much jocular laughter and ribbing.

'Africa,' whispered Verena, 'I am not sure I want to visit the Dark Continent! I have heard that it is a rough and dangerous place – '

Filled with fear, she crept back along the deck only to walk straight into the Captain.

"Jean."

81

"*Oui, Capitaine?*" answered Verena, terrified that the surly man was about to give her a dressing down for being above decks.

"A most agreeable breakfast, my lad. Now, if you will come with me, I have someone I wish you to meet. He is our new cabin boy and I hear he spent the past few days rolling around below deck being ill. No stomach, these young 'uns."

Verena concealed a smile with her hand. She thanked the Heavens that she had been blessed with a strong constitution.

She followed him to the bridge and there, in the corner, curled up in a ball on the floor was a boy of no more than fifteen. He was fast asleep, his mouth open and his dark hair all awry.

"Wake up, you good-for-nothing," yelled the Captain, Verena started, as did the boy. He yawned and stretched, then climbed slowly to his feet.

"Now, this here layabout is Pete. He's the cabin boy and by rights, he should be working with the Steward. Pete will come with you when we reach Gibraltar to help with carrying supplies. He's a small lad, I know, but strong. Pete, this here is the new chef, Jean. He's French, so mind he doesn't lose his temper with you."

Pete grinned and winked at Verena, who in turn, smiled back. She liked the look of this cheeky rascal, noticing that his cap was not straight and that he had a big white mark on the knee of his trousers.

"Pete will fetch anything you need from the hold and will carry any heavy objects," continued the Captain. "Any trouble, you come and tell me."

The Captain pushed Pete towards the door in an act of dismissal, so Verena followed.

"What do you want me to do first, then?" asked Pete cheekily, Verena thought long and hard.

"Take me to the hold," she decided at last. "I want to see what zere is on board."

"My pleasure. Follow me and mind your 'ead."

Verena was not sure if the boy was making fun of her, but as they descended into the bowels of the ship, she made up her mind to pay no heed to his jokes.

"Here we are," Pete announced finally.

Verena found herself standing in a dark and cold store room. Sacks were piled up next to boxes of tinned goods.

Her eyes gradually became adjusted to the dim light. Pete lit a candle and it threw strange shapes against the walls – the whole effect was rather eerie.

"I would like a sack of flour," said Verena after scanning the goods stacked up nearby.

"Is this your first voyage?" asked Pete, as he heaved the sack onto his back.

"No," replied Verena, forgetting her new persona. She hastily corrected herself. Zat is to say, I 'ave been on a boat across *La Manche*."

"Yer what?" asked Pete, his face a blank.

"Sorry, what is ze English word for it? The sea between England and France?"

"Oh, you mean the Channel," Pete informed her with a satisfied look on his face. "Pah, that don't count! Now me, I've been all over – France, Spain, the Americas."

"And still you have *le mal de mer*? Ze sea sickness?"

Verena gently teased.

Pete blushed to the roots of his hair.

"Well, it's these new steamships. I ain't used to them. Me, I love real ships, ones with sails. Real beauties."

Verena smiled to herself as they made their way back to the galley.

Pete was whistling to himself as they walked, a rather jaunty tune – it sounded like something that one might hear at a Music Hall, although Verena had never set foot in such a place.

Entering the galley, Pete threw the sack onto the floor.

"Right, I'll be off then, the Captain will want me to run errands for him."

Verena looked at the clock on the wall. There were still many long hours till luncheon. As there had been no word from the Marquis, she had decided upon a simple dish of grilled mackerel with mustard sauce served with cold potatoes and a small salad.

She stared at the wilting lettuce in the store cupboard. The day was another warm one.

'I must have some air,' she groaned.

Slipping out of the galley she made her way up to the deck.

'It will take me no time to make luncheon, I will not be missed for half-an-hour.'

Verena denied to herself the real reason for her sortie – deep inside she felt an overwhelming longing to steal a glimpse of the Marquis.

She walked quickly along the deck towards the Saloon. As she approached, she could see the door was open. Peeping inside, it was empty, save for Arthur who was busy laying the table for luncheon.

There was no sign of the Marquis.

Feeling disappointed, she proceeded along the deck towards the stern. Watching the water rushing behind them thrilled her.

Lost in thought, she was suddenly aware of a most peculiar sensation. The hairs on the back of her neck stood up – she could feel that someone was watching her!

She turned in time to see the Marquis heading off towards the bridge, his broad shoulders filling out a well-cut black jacket, his black hair ruffling in the wind.

Verena was filled with a sense of disappointment. She crept along the deck, hoping for another glimpse of him. As she passed the Saloon, she caught sight of someone inside.

'It is the Marquis,' she said to herself excitedly. 'If I stand here, I can watch him through the open door.'

The Marquis was standing at one of the many bookshelves where he selected a large volume bound in green leather and took it over to an easy chair.

Verena watched as he sank into the chair with a sigh and began to turn the creamy pages. He seemed engrossed as he continued to read.

She felt spellbound. Unsure of what it was that made her linger and stare.

'The mackerel can wait, just one minute more.' Just then, a piercing voice came from behind her and made her jump into the air.

"What-ho, there! Jean. I've got a sack of potatoes for you that I've just found in the hold. Shall I put them in the store cupboard?"

It was Pete, the cabin boy.

The Marquis heard the boy's voice and looked up in surprise to see his chef loitering around the Saloon door.

Verena blushed deeply as his eyes locked hers for the first time. It gave her such a strange sensation – her stomach wheeled and she felt quite light-headed.

"Why, Jean, I did not see you – have you been standing there for long?"

The Marquis shut his book, leaned forward and beckoned towards her.

"Do not be shy, come in. Was there something you wished to ask me? Perhaps you have a question about tonight's menu?"

"No – my Lord," stammered Verena, utterly embarrassed. "I was passing – and I saw ze door was open. I thought maybe – Monsieur Arthur was in here."

There was an agonising silence.

'What is wrong with me? Why can I not speak to this man?' she wondered, as the long seconds ticked by.

Pete the cabin boy was still at her elbow, holding the large sack of potatoes that smelt musty.

"Excuse me, my Lord," stammered Verena, before exiting swiftly with Pete running after her dragging the potatoes.

"Oi, wait for me!"

'What a curious fellow,' muttered the Marquis, as he resumed reading his book. 'I think he may be overawed by his new surroundings. Maybe he has not travelled by sea before.'

Below deck, Verena noisily banged her pots and pans furious at herself.

"I am an imbecile. A half-wit. Why could I just not talk to the man? What ails me?"

She shouted in French so that Pete could not understand her.

He stood in the corner, chuckling merrily at what he perceived was the chef having a tantrum.

"Well, I can't understand a word you're saying, but my, you sound very cross with someone. I hope it's not me," taunted Pete.

"*Tais-toi*!" screamed Verena, wishing she was not such a lady and could give in to her urge to throw something.

"Whoops! Better make myself scarce before that crate of mackerel lands on my head! I'll be with the Steward, if you need me."

Verena sat down and began to cry softly to herself. She could not understand why she felt as she did or why she was so upset that the Marquis had caught her watching him. Even though she had been warned that he liked his staff to be seen and not heard, he had not been unkind or harsh towards her –

'I must stop this foolishness at once,' she resolved.

*

The days passed and Verena found herself unable to resist creating opportunities to see the Marquis. Whether it was with some query on that evening's dinner or to find out which flavours pleased him.

She longed to pass comment on his library, and in particular, the books on Ancient Greece and Rome, but she dare not. She knew that no humble chef would be familiar with such titles and to express an interest would raise suspicion.

The weather grew warmer and she sensed the ship turning. The sun was now rising directly in front of them.

Verena asked one of the crew where they were and he grunted, "We be somewhere off the coast of Portugal and that there is Lisbon."

He waved his hand towards the horizon.

Verena stared hard and was sure she could just about make out the coastline. "Ar, I'll wager we'll dock in Gibraltar tomorrow mornin'."

"That soon?"

"Ar."

She felt a sudden sense of anticipation. Dry land! They had only been at sea for four days, but already she missed it. Much as she loved the swell of the ocean, she longed to see green trees and grass.

She could hardly sleep that night for excitement. After dinner had been cleared away and everyone had eaten their fill, she went up on deck.

It was a fine evening and the ship was gliding effortlessly through the water. The comforting chug of the engines and smell of coal enhanced the atmosphere.

She moved to return below deck as it was time she turned in. While she held the rails, she noticed a solitary figure standing on the top deck by the bridge. It was not the Captain, he was too tall.

'The Marquis! But what is he doing up there?'

He was looking intently out to sea. Although his back was to her, she could see that he was not moving a muscle.

'Why does he stand like that,' she wondered, 'he cannot possibly see anything, it is too far and too dark.'

It occurred to Verena that he held the air of a troubled man. Had she been able to see his face, she felt sure that she would have found his brow furrowed and his eyes full of conflict.

Once more, her heart surged out to him. She wished she could comfort him.

'But how can I? I am just a servant and one dressed as a boy at that. These feelings that I have for him are impossible, quite *impossible*!'

*

The next day dawned bright and sunny. There was a definite air of excitement around the ship as the crew made ready to dock in Gibraltar.

Pete was busy washing down the deck.

"Have to have it just so for his Lordship," he said as he scrubbed. "I want to make this deck as clean as my mother's neck. Ha, ha!"

Verena winced, the boy could be so crude and disrespectful – how he stayed out of trouble was a mystery to her.

"You are looking forward to coming ashore wiz me?" she enquired. Her voice low and gruff.

"Not 'alf. I'm going straight to the nearest tavern and ordering a foaming draft of ale."

Verena raised an eyebrow.

"Well, you will do zis without me, I do not care for alehouses."

"Ooh, what a toff," countered Pete.

She returned to the galley and began to prepare luncheon. The store cupboard was starting to look quite bare – but for some potatoes and pheasant, there would be no more meat for the table until she could find a suitable market.

Arthur arrived at midday ready to serve the meal.

"This is humble fare compared to what his Lordship has been eating," he commented, sliding the serving dishes onto the dumb waiter.

Verena shrugged.

"Zis evening I will make the big meal, but until I can go to the market, 'is Lordship will have to like it. I cannot magic a pig out of thin air!"

Arthur laughed gently.

"Now, wouldn't that be a thing if you could, Jean! I'd make my fortune out of you."

Verena instantly felt nervous – would the luncheon displease the Marquis? She grumbled to herself as she bustled around, making the pudding.

'I do hope not. But what can I do short of casting a line over the side and hoping to catch some of his precious octopus.'

She was suddenly aware of the ship pitching from side to side quite alarmingly. As she grabbed onto the countertop to steady herself, Jack appeared.

"Don't you fret, Jean. No need to look so scared.

We're just coming into port. It is always like this – cross currents, you see."

Verena nodded and felt her way along the counter to the dumb waiter, the strawberries in fruit jelly were wobbling wildly to one side and she wanted to get them onto the chute before they slid off.

The ship's engines roared beneath her feet and the ship lurched backwards.

"We're docking," shouted Jack.

Verena hastily pulled on the ropes and sent the strawberry confection hurtling upwards. She hoped that Arthur was still in the Saloon to receive it.

Sure enough, a few moments later, the dumb waiter ground into action and a selection of empty plates and the remains of the pheasant and potatoes appeared.

Verena noted with satisfaction that the Marquis had taken a fairly substantial portion. She would have difficulty in eking it out for the Captain and Arthur.

'For a troubled man, he has a healthy appetite,' she mused to herself.

Although she herself ate like a bird, as befitted a lady, she was appreciative of a man with a love of food.

Half an hour later she was walking down the gangway to the dock with Pete at her side wheeling a small handcart. His cap was set at a jaunty angle and he whistled all the while.

Verena was immediately overcome with the sights and sounds of Gibraltar.

In front of her everything seemed to be in the shadow of the Rock that loomed overhead. The port was much larger than Poole, she noted, and twice as busy.

They soon found the market. As it was so late, Verena was dismayed to find that much of the fresh fish had gone, but she did manage to purchase a small octopus and some fine-looking sardines, a local delicacy. The fisherman spoke English, as did many folk round about.

It did not take her long to fill Pete's cart and it was not without some persuasion that she pulled him away from a tavern not far from where the *Seahorse* was berthed.

"You must come back to the ship and 'elp me with the food," she instructed him.

Pete just sighed a merry twinkle in his black eyes.

"Right you are, but as soon as we've unloaded this little lot, I'm off! We're not sailing until tomorrow's tide, so that will give me plenty of time to sample Gibraltar's fine ales."

Verena shook her head and smiled to herself.

'He is such a lively fellow. I am so glad he is on board. I so enjoy being around him.'

It took her nearly two hours to put everything in its place. She carefully salted some pork she had found on a market stall and hung up a fine Spanish ham in the cool of the pantry.

There were crates of bright green vegetables, lemons and oranges with their leaves still attached, jars of fiery red pimenton made from sweet ground peppers and fat strands of ruby-red saffron, sacks of rice, juicy onions and large, knobbly garlic whose skin was still fresh and pliable.

She had not been able to resist a tray of dates from Morocco and had stocked up on almonds with which to stuff them for dessert.

'I will put a feast before the Marquis,' she vowed, pulling the octopus out of the bag to inspect it. The fisherman had given her precise instructions on how to prepare it – the dish was to be her *piece de resistance* tonight.

Arthur entered the galley, carrying an empty lemonade jug and glasses.

"Don't forget his Lordship has a guest this evening," he reminded her.

A cold hand of fear gripped Verena – she had put the guest to the back of her mind, not wishing to dwell on the fact that there may be a rival for her affections. She felt quite sick for a second and was forced to sit down.

Arthur raised an eyebrow and left the galley, obviously thinking she was having another tantrum.

'How foolish I am,' she admonished herself, 'how can this guest be a rival when the Marquis does not even know that I am not a boy! He could never fall in love with me whilst I am in disguise and it is quite the silliest notion for me to entertain.'

However sternly she talked to herself, she could not ignore the aching feeling in her heart.

As she bustled around the kitchen, trying hard to compose herself, there was a commotion over her head.

She could hear baggage being thrown into the hold and the cries of the crew as they ran hither and thither.

'It must be the Marquis's guest,' she thought with a sinking spirit. 'I must throw myself into my cooking. Tonight will be no different to any other night. In fact, I will make this meal extra special.'

Verena put her very heart and soul into the preparation of that night's dinner, a thousand wild thoughts chasing around her mind.

'And if I threw myself on his mercy and revealed myself?' she pondered, as she heated the new Spanish griddle she had bought, ready to throw on the onions and the octopus. 'What would he do? I could tell him I was fleeing in fear of my life – that is not so far from the truth – and perhaps he would take pity on me and forgive my deception.'

By the time she had sprinkled the last grains of salt on the octopus dish and added a good pinch of pimenton, she had convinced herself that she was nothing but a silly, addle-headed girl and that the best course of action was to keep quiet.

Just before the dessert of dates stuffed with almonds was served, Arthur appeared in the galley.

"My goodness, that tentacle stuff went down well," he said, sniffing appreciatively at the dates. "Mind you, just give me some of that ham and some fried potatoes for my dinner. I don't fancy what they ate. Too foreign for me, Jean."

Arthur's stoic Englishness made Verena laugh and forget her troubles. She passed him the salver of dates.

"I assure you, Arthur, I will be only too 'appy to fry you some potatoes."

"Good, glad to hear it. Now, let's get this lot upstairs. His Lordship is in a good mood this evening – must be his companion's influence."

His companion! Verena's heart sank to the very bottom of her boots. So it *was* a lady friend after all. She could not bear to ask Arthur for confirmation and she did not want to reveal herself to be that interested.

Slowly, she gathered up the dirty crockery. Jack had not appeared that evening, neither had Pete. The rest of the crew were most likely enjoying the benefits of being on land, so they would not miss the lack of supper.

Her appetite vanished. She was just about to retire to bed when Arthur appeared puffing and panting at the galley door.

"His Lordship wants you up in the Saloon right away."

"No, I cannot," she began.

"Don't worry," Arthur continued, "his Lordship is in fine fettle and he wants to speak to you personally about the meal and relay his compliments. Come on, don't dawdle, him and his guest are waiting."

Verena sighed and undid her apron. It was no use. She had to face whatever was about to happen.

She steeled herself as she followed Arthur up the stairs.

Her heart was beating so hard that she found herself short of breath.

The lights in the Saloon were very low – there was just one candelabra burning in the middle of the table.

As she approached, she could smell the Marquis's fine cigar and hear his voice rising in merriment.

'Laughter,' she thought, quite surprised. 'I have not heard him laugh once since we set off from Poole.' Arthur announced her arrival and he ushered her into the dark smoke-filled room.

As her eyes adjusted to the light, she could see the Marquis standing at the end of the table, a decanter of port in his hand.

"Ah, Jean," he said upon seeing her. "That was a most excellent meal – and you found me some octopus. Superb."

It was now Verena's turn to be unable to meet his gaze. She stood before him with her eyes cast downwards.

"We enjoyed it immensely," he continued, "you surpassed yourself, well done!"

Verena forced herself to look up, and as she did so, her eyes now used to the light, she glimpsed a figure seated at the dining table.

Her heart skipped a beat as not a woman, but a man loomed out of the darkness to light his cigar from one of the candles on the table.

"Hear, hear! Thumping good dinner," he added in staccato tones.

Verena could have fainted on the spot – the waxed whiskers and face red with good living were horribly familiar.

No, the truth behind the riddle of the Marquis's guest was far worse than a mere sweetheart – that she could have borne.

No, the man who stood before her, puffing contentedly on a cigar, was none other than Lord Mountjoy, one of her stepmother's closest friends from London!

He was a vile man who had made unwelcome advances to her during a brief visit to Rosslyn Hall not long after the new Countess had arrived. His lewd insinuations had deeply shocked her.

"May I present one of my oldest friends, Lord Mountjoy," exclaimed the Marquis.

96

Lord Mountjoy advanced towards Verena, locking eyes in a way that chilled her to the bone.

As the Marquis continued to speak, Lord Mountjoy's eyes never left her face. Verena felt hot then cold.

If there was one person in the entire world who could expose her as a fraud, it was he.

At last, he spoke directly to her, "D'you know, I have the darndest feeling that I know you from somewhere. Now, isn't that curious?"

The Marquis shrugged,

"I cannot see how, Jean has spent his life in France, studying fine cuisine. This is his first voyage out of that country – not unless he has a secret past he is concealing from us!"

The pair laughed heartily, Verena shuddered. She had the most terrible feeling that she was about to be unmasked.

As she stood under the unflinching gaze of Lord Mountjoy, she was hardly paying attention to what the Marquis was saying. There was an awkward silence and she realised that he had just addressed her.

"Jean?" he said, questioningly, "maybe I should speak in French, you may not have understood what I said."

"Don't go all *parlez-vous* on me, Jamie old boy," protested Lord Mountjoy. "You know I don't speak a darned word of the lingo!"

Verena looked shocked. It was the first time she had heard the Marquis's first name spoken. And to hear it said in such a cavalier way!

James! *James*. Such a sweet name!

The Marquis frowned at Lord Mountjoy. He obviously did not approve of such informality in front of the servants. Verena understood implicitly – had the same happened to her, she would have been most upset.

The Marquis turned to Verena and began to tell her in French that their next stop was Marseilles, a day or so away. She would have another chance to take on more provisions as they would then be sailing off into the Mediterranean and would not dock again for more than a week.

As he spoke, her heart fell into her boots. Two whole days.

The Marquis dismissed her from the room with a kindly wave of his hand, but Verena took no joy in his newfound bonhomie.

'Oh, what am I to do?' she howled to herself, as she ran along the deck. 'By the time we reach Marseilles, that awful man will have remembered who I am and will have me put ashore. I will be stranded. How can I stop him from finding out who I really am? I feel so alone. *What on earth am I to do*? I am at the mercy of that dreadful man!'

CHAPTER SEVEN

All that night, Verena lay awake on her bunk.

As the bells sounded for the last watch, she rose up and kissed the photograph of her mother.

'Oh, Mama, if only you were here. You would know what I must do to avoid being discovered.' She kissed the photograph once more with fervour before placing it back on the small cabinet by her bed.

Her eyes felt hollow and her mouth dry.

'I will go to the galley for a drink of water,' she decided.

Cautiously she dressed in her uniform before stealing out of her cabin.

'I do hope that everyone is asleep,' she thought as she slipped through the corridors. 'The Marquis and Lord Mountjoy were up rather late – they were playing music for hours after we had all gone to bed.'

The galley was strangely quiet when she reached it with only the purr of the engines beneath.

Verena helped herself to a glass of water and drank it standing up. She was just about to pour a second, when she heard a noise in the corridor outside.

Her heart missed a beat as she froze to the spot. Straining her ears she could distinctly hear shuffling noises – like someone in their slippers was kicking invisible dust.

'It must be Lord Mountjoy,' she thought to herself, in a panic. 'He has been lying in wait for me and now he's come to confront me!"

Verena stood terrified in the galley for quite some time. Eventually, she plucked up the courage to creep towards the door and peer down the corridor.

There was nothing and no one there.

She ran all the way back to her cabin, leaving her glass of water behind.

*

At around half-past six, Verena gave up any notion of sleeping. She arose from her bunk and looked at herself in the mirror. Her eyes were sunken with a black smudge under each one. Her skin was pasty and drawn.

'I am glad that no one expects me to look decorative,' she mused as she left her cabin once more for the galley. 'Today I am grateful for being just a chef and not a lady on constant display.'

Once there she took down the book of menus and scanned the pages.

'Alas, there is not enough fruit for me to make a salad or *compote* and I so wanted to present something different for breakfast this morning.'

She closed the book of menus in despair. Nothing had inspired her.

Just then, Pete walked in, yawning and tousle-haired, looking as if he had literally just fallen from his bunk.

"Morning, Jean. Cor, I don't 'alf 'ave a thumpin' 'ead this morning!"

His dancing black eyes were sunken into his face and as he came closer, Verena could smell the odour of stale ale and smoke upon him.

"Pfft! Go away," she said, wrinkling her nose, "you smell 'orrible!"

"Now, now, take pity on a boy. I'm dying of thirst. Do you have any of that lemonade you made yesterday?"

Verena opened up the store cupboard door and peered inside. On a shelf in the middle was a jug covered with muslin. Lemons floated sadly around inside.

Pete took the jug and poured himself a large glass. In seconds, it had disappeared.

"Do you know what I fancy now?" he said, wiping his mouth on his sleeve, "some of those fancy sweet rolls you get on the Continent."

"Why, of course!" exclaimed Verena, "*merci* Pete, *merci beaucoup*," she ran over to the boy and hugged him.

"Woah! Steady on," Pete recoiled in horror.

"I am sorry, I should explain," she responded, as she began to take down flour and yeast from the shelf.

"I did not know what to make for 'is Lordship's breakfast and now, you 'ave given me an idea."

Pete smiled and left the galley, a baffled look on his face.

'I have time enough before his Lordship rises,' thought Verena, as she proved the dough in the warm stove. 'He will be eating fresh croissants and brioches this morning. There are some preserves in the store cupboard and I can also serve some cheese and ham – *parfait*!'

Soon the galley was filled with the inviting smell of baking.

Arthur came in, his face the picture of ecstasy.

"Mmm, now that smells like a breakfast worth waiting for," he commented, sniffing the air greedily. "What are you baking, Jean?"

"It is croissants and brioche, *formidable, non?*"

"Whatever they are, they smell delicious."

Verena took the first tray of brioche out of the oven – they were golden brown and inviting.

Suddenly feeling quite hungry, she could not resist the temptation and took one hot from its mould and popped it into her mouth.

"Naughty, naughty!" cried Arthur, a mock disapproving look on his face. "I'll tell his Lordship that you were sampling the goods before him."

Verena and Arthur burst into gales of hearty laughter, but the joyous mood was abruptly curtailed when the galley door suddenly flew open and there stood Lord Mountjoy.

"Ah, so this is where you hide yourself!" he bawled, his beady eyes scouring the galley before sweeping over a terrified Verena. "Thought I'd just get my bearings and I couldn't help but follow my nose."

He walked over to the tray of hot brioches and took one, cramming it into his red mouth greedily.

Both Verena and Arthur were rooted to the spot. Of course, neither could make any comment on the man's rude behaviour as he was their better.

Verena felt sick, the brioche she had just eaten was fast curdling in her stomach.

"Quite delicious," pronounced Lord Mountjoy, his eyes never leaving Verena's face. "Where was it again you said you trained?"

"It – it was near Orly," stammered Verena, terrified of his stare.

There was a long silence as his eyes continued to bore into her.

"Splendid," he announced, brushing crumbs from his moustache before leaving the galley without uttering another word.

"He seems a bit of a rum 'un," remarked Arthur, wiping his brow, "and he doesn't seem to like you very much, Jean. Have you two met before?"

Verena hated to tell a lie, but she had to.

"*Non*," she replied, her head drooping. "I do not know zis man."

"Well, I wouldn't like to get on the wrong side of him," he continued, "and he's not such a gentleman as he seems."

"Why you say zis?"

Arthur lowered his voice and moved closer to her with a conspiratorial air.

"Much as I hate servant's gossip," he began, "but I have heard that Lord Mountjoy is a bit of a cad."

Lowering his voice to a whisper, he continued, "It is rumoured that he, erhem, compromised a young lady in Bath. Her reputation was naturally ruined and she was forced to leave for Africa to become a missionary. Now, what do you think of that?"

Verena was unsure how to reply. This after all was just mere servant's hearsay, but equally she knew that there would be much more than a grain of truth in it.

She shrugged her shoulders dismissively.

"I do not know if zis is true, but that Lord Mountjoy, 'e makes me feel, how you say, not easy?"

"You mean, ill at ease?" Arthur nodded sagely. "Yes, I agree, a most shifty fellow. Yet the Marquis is his friend and this is not the first time we have had the man on board and the last trip he caused no end of fuss. He pretends not to recognise me, but I know him. Oh, yes!"

The rest of the morning passed without further incident. Not a crumb of breakfast was left and the Marquis called Verena to the saloon wishing to relay his compliments.

Although Verena was thrilled to be summoned again, it was with fear in her heart that she entered the Saloon.

As she gingerly knocked and waited for the Marquis's warm voice to beckon her enter, she felt sick with anxiety.

"Ah, Jean," beamed the Marquis as she entered. "I enjoyed your surprise of serving us French pastries for breakfast. Most delightful and tasty. It provided a welcome change from your usual fare."

Verena was unable to reply. She simply nodded and averted her eyes.

Once more, she was aware that Lord Mountjoy was staring at her hard. Without even looking up, she could tell he was feverishly racking his brain for some clue as to where he had seen this chef before.

"May I go, my Lord?" she finally asked. "There is much to prepare for luncheon."

"Of course, make it a light one, Jean. I fear I will still be too full of pastries to eat much. Maybe a salad and some cold cuts?"

"*Tres bien*, my Lord."

As Verena left the saloon, it was as if she had two hot knives probing her back.

'I will stay below deck as much as I can,' she resolved as she returned to the galley. 'The more that man sees me, the better chance he has of remembering where he has seen my face before.'

*

The two days en route to Marseilles seemed to Verena to pass as slowly as would a week.

She tried to keep below decks, but the heat of the galley occasionally became too much for her and she was forced to seek some fresh air.

On the few occasions when she went up on deck, inevitably, Lord Mountjoy would appear, watching and scrutinising.

Verena began to feel hunted. She ate even less than usual and carried on with her duties without taking any joy in them.

"Is everything all right with you?" enquired Arthur on the morning that they were due to dock in Marseilles.

"Why do you ask?" replied Verena, warily, as she stirred a pan of browning onions. She was making a French onion soup for luncheon.

"If you don't mind me saying, you have not been yourself for these past few days."

Verena sighed and said nothing.

"We dock in Marseilles this afternoon, perhaps being back in your homeland will cheer you up."

"*Oui, oui*," replied Verena thinking, 'if only he knew. France is not my homeland at all, but England. How far away it now seems. It is as if I lived there in another lifetime.'

*

Luncheon was uneventful. Thankfully the Marquis simply conveyed his compliments via the Steward and did not request her presence upstairs. She contented herself with making a list of provisions that she and Pete would need to purchase for the long voyage ahead.

Normally she would have looked forward to a sortie on shore, but she found herself filled with dread at the prospect, certain that Lord Mountjoy would find a way of dogging her every step.

She was just finishing her list when Arthur appeared.

"His Lordship and his guest will be disembarking at Marseilles and visiting the British Consulate," he announced.

"Both of them?"

"Perhaps they both have business with the Consul, I don't know."

Verena was once again gripped with the most awful cold fear. The British Consulate. That could mean only one thing. No doubt, Lord Mountjoy would inform them that she was aboard and would exhort them to get in contact with her father.

It would be only a matter of time now before they came to find her and pack her off back home.

'I cannot let this happen,' she said to herself, 'but all is not yet lost. I must think of a way out, should I be discovered.'

It was nearly two o'clock and luncheon had long since finished when she heard the shouts of the crew overhead as they made ready to dock at Marseilles.

Pete had joined her in the galley, hoping to duck out of the more strenuous duties involved in steering a steamship across the bay to drop anchor.

"Show me your list then," he teased, trying to peer over her shoulder. "What marvellous items have I to hike back to the ship this time? Half a walrus, maybe? A ton of dried elephant's tongue?"

His jocular air soothed Verena and made her smile for the first time in some days.

"*Mais oui*, Pete, and I will make you taste it all before I buy!"

They both laughed as the boy pulled a horrified face.

Overhead they could hear the running of feet and the shouts of the men.

"We must have docked," said Pete, "come on, Jean, let's go and find the cart and be on our way."

Verena could not help looking over her shoulder as they rolled it down the gangway. Although the day was hot and fine, there was quite a breeze and the flimsy gangway rocked from side to side making it difficult to handle the cart.

Halfway down, Pete nearly lost his footing.

"Phew! Thought I was about to go into the drink," he groaned as they pulled the cart off the gangway.

As they visited shop after shop, she could not shake off the feeling that she was being followed.

'I am being most foolish,' she told herself, as they made their way through the winding streets of Marseilles, 'Lord

107

Mountjoy has gone to the Consulate with the Marquis. He will not have taken the trouble to follow me. Besides, I have Pete with me and he would not dare to make a move whilst he is by my side.'

Her thoughts were interrupted by Pete, shouting at her from the other side of the street, "Here, Jean. Look at these."

Pete was standing outside a *boulangerie* that was piled high with loaves of every shape and description. He was pointing to a tray of pastries that were baked in the shape of small boats.

"They are called *navettes*," she explained, "which means little boats."

"Can you go inside and buy a couple for me?" asked Pete, diving into his pocket for some coins. "I think I have a franc or two from my last visit, I must show them to the lads on board."

Verena took the money and went inside. She asked the woman behind the counter about the strangely shaped pastries and she immediately launched into a long explanation.

After more than ten minutes of listening patiently while the woman chattered on interminably about Lazarus and little boats, Verena managed to pay for the pastries and politely take her leave.

But once outside the shop, there was no sign of Pete or the handcart full of her shopping.

She stood in the street unable to find her bearings. They had wandered all over this part of Marseilles for quite some time and she had long since lost any sense of where the docks might be situated.

'I shall wait here for a while,' she decided, 'Pete will surely be back presently.'

But she waited for a good fifteen minutes to no avail. Sighing, she picked up her basket and began to walk.

The sun was sinking slowly but burned no less fierce. She judged it to be around four o'clock and many shops were showing signs of closing for the day.

She walked and walked but could not find Pete.

'I will have to return to the ship,' Verena resolved.

But that was easier said than done as she soon discovered. All the streets looked the same after a while – the same overhanging buildings with the same shutters – and she found herself back where she had started some ten minutes previously.

Sighing with impatience, she suddenly had the feeling that there was someone behind her. She could hear no footfalls – rather it was just a sense of being followed.

She quickened her pace and changed her direction. But still she felt pursued.

Time and time again, she glanced over her shoulder. Just once, she swore she saw a figure ducking into a doorway with a large porch.

She waited. Every last hair on her head standing on end. Her body tense and ready to flee – but no one appeared to be anywhere in the street.

Just then, a cat crossed the road and Verena heaved a sigh of relief. It must have been the animal that she had sensed in pursuit.

'That will be it! I have fish in my basket and it has a strong enough smell to have half of the cats of Marseilles after me.' On she trudged, making very little progress.

Turning a corner, she spied an ironmonger's shop that had yet to close for the day. She crept inside and asked the proprietor for directions to the port.

In a strong Marseilles accent, he told her that she was not far – then drew her a map on a brown paper bag.

"*Merci beaucoup*, monsieur," Verena thanked him, clutching her makeshift map to her breast. "*Merci, mille fois.*"

She left the shop feeling light of heart. So light, in fact, that she failed to notice the shadowy figure creeping around the corner of a nearby alleyway –

Verena looked at her map one more time and sighed,

'Now, if I can find the monument, then the docks should be not far away.'

She did not know what it was that made her quicken her pace – perhaps it was some sixth sense – but she suddenly had the distinct feeling once more of being followed.

Her heart beat faster as she ran through the streets, trying to shake off her pursuer.

A thousand thoughts were streaming through her mind. Was it a criminal who followed her? A madman with a knife?

Suddenly, a man grabbed her from behind, his hand clamped fast over her mouth as he dragged her into a dark alley. As he pulled her backwards, Verena could see that the road ahead opened out into the docks.

"Very clever, young lady. Very clever indeed," came a hissing voice.

Verena tried to struggle, but the man held her tight in his grip.

"It has finally come to me who you are and I know a certain Countess of my acquaintance from Hampshire, who will reward me handsomely for the return of her runaway stepdaughter!"

"Lord Mountjoy!" she cried, "I beg of you, let me go."

Lord Mountjoy laughed. With one swift movement, he let go and then tied up her wrists behind her back.

Verena was almost swooning from fear.

"Now, tell me. What is there to stop me from putting you on the boat back to England?" he snarled.

"I beg you, please, let me go," repeated Verena, tears falling from her eyes. Her basket lay in the gutter, its contents scattered. The *navettes* she had bought Pete were crushed to crumbs under Lord Mountjoy's feet.

His eyes glittered with a reptilian air as he watched her on her knees and crying. No sign of mercy was to be found in their cold depths.

"I will do anything, but I cannot go back to England."

"Yes, and I know precisely why. Your father was furious when he discovered that you had run away. Couldn't find a thing out from anyone – the servants closed ranks and refused to talk. He has dismissed your maid, you know."

Verena was desperate to find out if he had done the same with Barker, but she knew she could not ask.

Lord Mountjoy regarded her for a long moment. He licked his lips before saying,

"Of course, there is one way I could be persuaded to forget I know that you are none other than Lady Verena Rosslyn, and not some poor chef from Orly –"

Verena looked up at him, hoping to find some sign of mercy in those cold, cold eyes.

"And that is come away with me! I had not necessarily intended to sail on the *Seahorse* to its next destination and it would be easy for both of us to disappear here. I could tell the Marquis that his precious chef has been thrown into jail. After all, we are in France and chefs are ten a penny here."

"I am sorry, I do not understand what you mean," Verena replied, still on her knees. "Come away with you? For what purpose?"

Lord Mountjoy let out a long cruel laugh.

"Why, quite the innocent aren't we?" he chuckled, "my dear, I am hardly inviting you to tea at Fortnum and Mason's. I am suggesting that if you were to become my mistress, then I would be inclined to help you, rather than be the cause of your undoing."

Verena stared at him in utter horror.

"Your mistress! Never, never, never! I would rather die!"

Lord Mountjoy smiled again,

"With the fate that awaits you in the arms of the Duke of Dalkenneth, I would wager that death would be the more pleasant option," he sneered. "You should consider most carefully my gracious offer. A house in London, all the gowns and jewels you would wish for, holidays in Monte Carlo and Florence and no one need know of your current plight."

'I am trapped,' thought Verena to herself, 'if I do not agree, this man will unmask me to the Marquis and he will surely have me arrested for deception. The very best I can hope for is that he puts me off the ship here in Marseilles – I simply cannot agree to be Lord Mountjoy's mistress! I cannot, oh, *I cannot*!'

"I see you are having some trouble making your mind up, Lady Verena," Lord Mountjoy taunted her. "Well consider this. A Marseilles jail is no place for a lady – especially for one who is posing as a boy. Make the wrong decision now and his Lordship will surely have you thrown into one immediately. He cannot bear to be deceived –"

Verena remained silent. Surely she had not misjudged the Marquis that he was capable of such action?

Lord Mountjoy pulled her up from her knees and began to drag her in the direction of the docks.

"We will see what a few hours in your cabin will do for your powers of decision making," he smirked.

The *Seahorse* was deserted when the pair arrived back to where the ship was berthed. The only sound was the creaking of the rope that tied the ship to the dock.

Lord Mounjoy pushed Verena up the gangway and down the stairs leading to the lower decks.

Verena prayed with all her might that Arthur or Pete might suddenly appear and come to her aid, but there was no one around.

Reaching her cabin, Lord Mountjoy pushed open the door and shoved Verena inside so hard that she hit her bunk.

He was breathing heavily as he looked at her – tears were running down her cheeks, her eyes wide with fear.

"Such a pretty face, such a pity to have cut off all your lovely hair –"

He ran his fingers through her shorn locks, a strange look on his face.

Verena turned sharply away. Her skin crawled at his very touch.

'What is he about to do?' she shuddered anxiously, as his fingers hovered over her cheek. 'Surely he would not try to take advantage of me whilst enjoying the hospitality of the Marquis?'

As if he read her thoughts, Lord Mountjoy began to caress her cheek.

Verena felt sick to her very stomach. She closed her eyes and tried to move away.

But he gripped her face hard, pulling her towards him.

Verena could smell his breath – it reeked of stale cigarettes, fish and garlic.

'*Moules*,' she thought with disgust.

"You will submit to me," murmured Lord Mountjoy, his lips moving towards hers.

With all the strength that she could muster, Verena brought her feet up sharply and kicked him as hard as she could.

In the struggle that ensued, he ripped her shirt, exposing her chemise underneath.

Hearing the fabric tear, he pulled back and looked at Verena, red-faced and panting. Her eyes were filled with hatred.

Softly laughing to himself, Lord Mountjoy got up and released her.

"No, I will not rush into taking my prize," he declared, straightening his jacket.

"I will give you until six o'clock to make your mind up. Should you decide to refuse my offer, I will have no choice but to reveal to the Marquis who you are. Let us see how a couple of hours of contemplation will soften your attitude."

He took the key out of the lock and slammed the door behind him. Verena could hear the key turning and then Lord Mountjoy's footsteps as he departed along the corridor.

She began to weep once more. What could she do?

Her hands were still fastened tight behind her and even if she had been free, she could not have escaped from the cabin.

She thought of crying out – but there was no one on board, apart from Lord Mountjoy, to hear her.

Verena glanced over at the photograph of her mother.

'Oh, Mama. *Help me*. Please help me if you can. My very life is in peril!' But no answer came.

She became increasingly desperate. In the distance, she heard a Church clock strike four and then the half hour.

'I must think of something, I *must*.' There were noises overhead and Verena guessed that some of the crew had returned. She thought she could hear Pete's muffled tones, laughing as always and making jokes.

But even if she cried out, how could he hear her with so much metal between them? He would simply attribute her screams to the screeching of gulls overhead.

'I have to think of another way,' she decided. 'I do not have much time left. Lord Mountjoy will be returning soon.'

115

Weary with shock and thoroughly exhausted, Verena began to doze. As she gave herself up to sleep, she came to a decision.

'Perhaps there is no other way but to confess all to the Marquis. I have to be brave and trust him. I have no other alternative. For better or for worse I must throw myself at his mercy – '

As she slept on, so tired was she that the sound of footsteps fast approaching her cabin failed to wake her –

CHAPTER EIGHT

As Verena slept on, she began to dream.

In her dream, she imagined that she was on a ship – one not unlike the *Seahorse* – and she was trapped below deck desperately trying to find a way out. She was no longer Jean the chef – she was herself once more and as she ran, she constantly tripped up on the hem of her dress.

In the distance, she could hear music. She knew that for some reason she had to find its source, but try as she might, she could not locate where it was coming from.

Every door she opened, there was nothing but an empty cabin in front of her.

She became more and more agitated and began to cry.

Suddenly out of nowhere a black cat appeared chasing a mouse along one of the corridors. Curious, she followed it and in a flash, the cat lost interest in the mouse and instead wound its furry body around Verena's legs. It seemed to want her to follow it as it pawed at her skirts and mewed entreatingly. It led Verena to a door she had not seen before.

The cat came to a halt and began to wash itself. Verena wasted no time, pushing the door. It flew open and there before her was a set of steps.

The sound of music was growing closer. Verena hurriedly ascended the stairs.

But the stairs went on forever. Just as she thought she had reached the top, another flight of stairs rolled out in front of her.

At the very top, she could see the tall, elegant figure of the Marquis. He was reaching out to her, calling her name, "Verena, dearest! Come, be my love," he cried.

But try as she might, Verena could not reach the top of the stairs.

"I love you! Wait for me," she shouted, as she ran up yet another flight on the never ending staircase – Suddenly, there was a series of loud bangs and it all went dark.

*

Verena gradually emerged from her dream, aware that the loud bangs in her dream were in fact someone knocking hard on her cabin door.

'Lord Mountjoy,' she moaned to herself, fearfully. 'He has returned to torment me.'

Then she realised that he had a key and would have had no need of knocking.

"Jean! Jean. Are you in there?" came a muffled voice. "The Marquis wants to see you."

Verena was too exhausted to answer. She heard the far-off Church clock strike five and next the sound of footsteps receding back up the corridor.

She lay in silence, shaken by her strange dream. The realisation dawning on her that her words to the Marquis rang horribly true. In spite of trying to deny it to herself, she was indeed in love with him.

Yes, *she loved him*!

'But it is hopeless,' she sighed, 'the best I can hope for is that he treats me with clemency and pays me the money I have earned so far. Then at least I will have a chance of finding sanctuary elsewhere. Perhaps I could take a train to Switzerland and find work teaching cookery to young ladies in Geneva – '

Her thoughts was interrupted by the unmistakeable sound of a key in the lock.

'Lord Mountjoy!' she shrieked, 'Oh, may the Heavens have mercy on me.'

The door sprang open and there, with anxious expressions on their faces, were Arthur and Pete.

Their looks of anxiety soon turned to ones of horror as they took in the sight of Verena, her face filthy and tear stained, her shirt torn clearly showing the white cotton chemise underneath.

"Blimey!" exclaimed Pete, "Jean's a girl!"

"Now you just keep your mouth shut and come and help me," shouted Arthur. "Some blackguard has tied the poor thing up – look!"

He pointed to the rough rope that cut into Verena's delicate wrists.

"I'll fetch the Captain," suggested Pete.

"You'll do no such thing, young man, keep watch at the door and I'll help the young lady." He produced the knife that he used to cut the seals on wine bottles and began to saw at the rope.

"Thank you, thank you," whispered Verena.

She was close to fainting with relief that it was her friend Arthur who had found her and not Lord Mountjoy.

With the rope cut, Verena sat up and rubbed her aching wrists. Arthur respectfully averted his eyes whilst she pulled on a robe that was draped over the bed.

"Now, I think you had better tell me what has happened from the beginning."

Verena's eyes filled with fear. She wanted to speak but found that no sound came from her mouth.

"Now don't worry, you are quite safe. Pete won't let anyone past – not even a pack of rabid dogs!"

Arthur moved and sat himself down on the chair at the foot of the bed, keeping a respectful distance. He knew instinctively that he was in the presence of a lady – no matter what she may have called herself previously – and that he should treat her accordingly.

Drying her tears, Verena began to tell her tale.

"My name is Lady Verena Rosslyn. My father, the Earl, recently remarried after my own dear mother had died six years ago. My new stepmother thought that it was high time that I was married and without any regard for my wishes, took it upon herself to select a husband for me. I was to have no choice in the matter."

Arthur shook his head. The story was touching him deeply.

"I did not think that arranged marriages of this sort were still common practice, my Lady. So many gentlemen and ladies marry for love nowadays that I believed the old ways had died out."

"Had it been left to my father, he would have been happy to have allowed me to follow my heart," continued Verena, "but now he is in thrall of his new wife and so supported her belief that I was too old to be unmarried."

"Sounds like she wanted you off her hands," commented Arthur.

"You speak the truth, Arthur. She has one goal and one goal only and that is to drive me away from Rosslyn Hall. I knew that I could not bear to marry a man I did not love, so I ran away."

"A very brave course of action, my Lady."

"It was either that or face a living death as the wife of a cold cruel man who wants no more than a vessel to provide him with an heir. My mother and father married for love and were extremely happy – had my mother been alive she would never have allowed such a turn of events to be put into motion."

"So you ran away to sea. But how did you come to pose as a boy?" asked Arthur intrigued.

Verena pulled from the cabinet the creased sailor's uniform she had bought in Poole.

"I tried to board a ship to France, which I know quite well as I went to finishing school in Paris. That much of my 'false life' is true. But none were sailing in time for me to make an escape before my father came after me. I saw the notice advertising the post of chef for the *Seahorse*, but was turned down by the clerk at the counter. He informed me that his Lordship, the Marquis, refused to have women on board –
"

Arthur hesitated and drew a sharp breath.

"Well, that much is true, my Lady. I have served his Lordship for ten years on his ships and he has never allowed a female to set foot on the deck."

Verena looked at him, searchingly.

"Do you know why?"

"I'm afraid not. His Lordship is not accustomed to sharing his thoughts and feelings with his servants. His father passed away a few years back and he has increasingly sought solitude. Lord Mountjoy has been the first guest on the *Seahorse* since his Lordship's father was alive – they were at boarding school together. Anyway, my Lady, you have not finished telling me your story. We can speak about the Marquis later."

Once more, Verena took up the story.

"When the clerk refused me on the grounds of my sex, I hatched a plot. I recalled the story of how Joan of Arc was forced to dress as a boy to join the French army and afterwards led them to victory – so I followed her example.

I bribed a sailor boy to sell me a uniform. I cut off my hair and then returned to the ticket office to make enquiries about the job.

"It was an easy matter for me to change my voice and adopt a French accent – I lived in Paris for over a year just after my mother died and I used to take much pleasure in imitating the pigeon English of my teachers. The clerk did not even look at me twice. He directed me to the *Seahorse*. I had to cook a dish for the Captain and here I am!"

"But your clothes are ripped. Pete told us that he lost you in the maze of streets and decided to head back to the ship. He arrived back on board some hours ago – before the Marquis requested that I fetch you to discuss this evening's meal. I was worried sick when you didn't return. So tell me, what happened? And why were you tied up in your cabin? It just doesn't make sense to me, unless I am missing a clue –"

Arthur stared hard at Verena, but it was with the caring air of a father, rather than the scrutiny of a persecutor.

Seeing his concern, she began to cry. It had been a long while since she felt that anyone had been concerned for her well-being.

"I cannot tell you. It is too awful!"

"But, my Lady, you are lucky that you were not seriously injured or worse – " His voice trailed off. "You must tell me who has done this to you and the authorities must be informed."

Verena's tears turned to sobs.

Arthur watched in alarm as her slender body shuddered with emotion. He would have comforted her as Jean, but could not now that he knew who she really was.

Then a sudden realisation dawned on him as he recalled the events of the past few days. That incident in the galley with the brioche!

"Lord Mountjoy," he blurted out.

There was a long silence during which nothing but Verena's whimpers could be heard. With full eyes, she looked up at Arthur and simply nodded her affirmation.

"The cad! The utter cad!" he screamed, his face contorted with anger. "I knew that one was no gentleman."

"I have indeed encountered Lord Mountjoy before," admitted Verena, "it was not long after my father brought Lady Louisa back to Rosslyn Hall as his new wife. My stepmother immediately threw a party for her intimates and Lord Mountjoy was amongst the guests. He pursued me for his entire stay, and made certain suggestions –"

"Under the very nose of your father? The man is a no-good –"

Verena silenced him with a look.

"That may be as well, but I had not given it another thought until his arrival onboard the *Seahorse*. I had believed that the Marquis's guest was to be his sweetheart! I could never have imagined that such a fine man would have such a loathsome creature as a friend."

"And the incident in the galley?"

"That was his way of trying to intimidate me. The first time I was introduced to him, Lord Mountjoy declared that he found my face familiar but could not recall from where. Although I could fool others in my disguise as a French chef, I had not counted on having to deceive someone who knew me. It was only a matter of time before Lord Mountjoy remembered where he had seen my face before, and after that, he sought to blackmail me with a most improper suggestion."

"My Lady?" queried Arthur.

Verena took a deep breath, unsure as to whether she should share the full awful truth with Arthur, but her future depended on him, so she composed herself and continued, "He followed me when Pete and I went ashore to buy provisions. We got lost in the maze of streets and we became separated.

"As I tried to find my way back to the ship, Lord Mountjoy pounced and threatened to unmask me to the Marquis and have me packed off back to England in return for a reward from the Countess. He knew of my disappearance and seized on a chance encounter as a way of making money.

"Oh, I cannot say what he suggested, but it would have meant the ruination of me. My reputation would have been in tatters. He brought me back here and tried to assault me, then locked me up, saying that if I didn't submit to his wishes, he would go to the Marquis and reveal me as a liar and an impostor. I have no wish to end up in a Marseilles jail. Arthur, what shall I do?"

Arthur sat and fumed silently.

"His Lordship must be told about this. I cannot stand to be under the same roof as that snake Mountjoy."

"No, no, you must not."

"Why ever not? His Lordship is a complete gentleman and would not hesitate to defend a lady's honour."

"Even a lady who has deceived him into believing that she was a boy and a trained chef? And who had sought employment with him under false pretences?" whispered Verena.

"His Lordship is an upstanding gentleman and a most compassionate one. Whilst it is true that he can appear aloof and unfriendly – he's the very devil for not meeting your gaze – he has a strong sense of justice and hates to see cruelty of any kind. I once saw him whip a man who had set about a lame horse. By Jove, he gave that fellow a sound thrashing. 'See how you like it,' he said."

"But this is not the same as a lame horse being thrashed," she replied. "I have lied to him. Surely, he will not overlook that?"

"His Lordship has a forgiving nature. My Lady, you have no choice, he must be informed at once of what has happened with Lord Mountjoy. He is under no illusions as to his character."

Verena felt utterly torn. She wanted so much to trust the Marquis – her love for him was inclining her to beg for his compassion, but she ran the risk of losing him altogether if she confessed all.

Would a man such as he view her as spoilt goods after the day's events?

Could he ever love a woman whom Lord Mountjoy had pursued?

"He is returning at six o'clock for my decision," explained Verena, "if I do not comply with his demands, he will have me arrested."

"Pardon me, my Lady, but I do not think his Lordship would gladly suffer a swarm of French policemen running over the *Seahorse*. It would cause a scandal. No, you have to tell him exactly what you have told me – with respect, my Lady, there is no other way."

Long minutes passed by whilst Verena considered what Arthur had said.

'If I appeal to his good nature, then maybe all will be well,' she told herself. 'But I do not think I will be able to stand it should he dismiss me. The thought of never seeing him again tears me in two. Oh, how I love him!'

Arthur waited patiently until finally Verena spoke,

"I have come to a decision. I will tell the Marquis," she announced. "Now, if you would kindly leave the cabin for ten minutes, I will change and make myself presentable.

Would you please speak to Pete and ask him to keep quiet about me?"

"I'll try my best, my Lady. I may have to threaten him but rest assured, if I have to sew his mouth up myself, I will obtain his silence."

Arthur left the cabin and as Verena filled the small sink with water from the jug, she could hear him outside, talking to Pete in a low voice. It comforted her to know that she was being guarded.

'I will do my utmost to make a good impression on the Marquis,' she resolved, her heart in her mouth.

She pulled her small suitcase and vanity case out from under the bunk. Opening the suitcase, the smells of home wafted out and made her feel quite homesick once again.

She shook out her fine muslin dress and held it against her figure.

'It is quite crumpled, but at this moment that is not important.' She laid it on the bed and took a cake of soap from her vanity case. The packet was quite worn, but the soap still retained the smell of lavender.

Moving over to the sink, Verena lathered up the soap. She then stripped down to her undergarments and washed.

Pulling on her dress, she noticed that she had lost weight, as it had been quite tight the last time she had worn it. Now it fitted her perfectly.

She gazed anxiously in the mirror as she vigorously scrubbed her face until her cheeks shone pink, but there was nothing she could do with her badly cut hair. It hung in hanks across her face and would not sit smoothly.

Smoothing down her dress, she attempted to view her reflection in the tiny mirror.

'It's no use, I will have to go as I am to the Marquis and hope that the sight of me will not displease him too much.'

Her heart was beating hard as she opened the door to the cabin. Pete and Arthur stood outside waiting for her.

"Well, there's a sight for sore eyes and make no mistake," whistled Pete,

"Mind your manners, boy," admonished Arthur.

Pete bobbed a curtsy.

"Sorry, my Lady!"

Verena smiled as the rascal winked at her. If she was to leave, she would be sorry to not see Pete again. He was such a lively fellow.

"Arthur, let's go and find the Marquis without further delay," suggested Verena, her stomach churning at the mere thought of seeing him dressed as she was.

"Right away, my Lady."

"Lord Mountjoy is in for a shock," added Pete, mischievously.

"Now hush, what did I tell you?" said Arthur, a stern look on his face.

Arthur led the way along the corridor and up the stairs to the deck. Verena could scarcely breathe as they approached the Saloon.

As agreed, Arthur was to knock, enter and announce her as Jean. She would then walk in and give herself up to her fate.

Verena could hear the soft strains of Bach wafting out of the saloon door.

Arthur paused before knocking and nodded at Verena.

"Please proceed," she said quietly her legs feeling quite unsteady under her muslin dress.

He knocked and waited. After a few moments, the Marquis bid him enter.

"Your Lordship – the chef."

"Ah, thank you, Arthur. Bring him in."

As Verena crept through the door, she saw that the Marquis had his back to her. He was taking a disc off the gramophone and polishing its surface with a cloth.

Sensing her presence in the room, he turned around, the record still in his hand.

When he caught sight of Verena standing there in her white muslin dress, her face shining with hope and her short dark hair so fetchingly caught up behind her ears, he could not conceal his shock and bewilderment.

For a tense moment, he simply stood by the gramophone with a puzzled look on his face.

Next he took a deep breath and spoke – the words came out hesitantly, "Well, for the first time in my life words desert me! Am I to understand that my chef is not a man but a woman? Arthur? Can you explain this apparent aberration?"

Arthur stepped forward from the side of the room and coughed, "I think my Lady can tell you better than I. May I beg to be excused?"

The Marquis nodded, dazzled by the vision in white who stood before him.

Such was the silence that Verena threw herself to her knees at the Marquis's feet.

"Please, I entreat you. Do not throw me off the ship. My life is in your hands, I am totally at your mercy. I beg of you, please do not hand me over to the authorities. I cannot go back to England! *I cannot!*"

The Marquis, somewhat dazed, took Verena by the hand and pulled her to her feet.

"Well, I must declare I had thought that there was something a trifle odd about you, but I had attributed that to your being unused to such surroundings."

He gestured around the room. In the late afternoon light, the room appeared no less rich and sumptuous than it had in the warm candle light of evening.

"Now, please be seated and tell me your story. It must be an intriguing one indeed for you to pass yourself off as a boy when it is quite apparent now that you are a lady of fine breeding. Do you really think that I am about to throw such a divine cook off my ship?"

He stared at Verena, his warm amber eyes searching deep within hers.

"I don't know – " she started haltingly.

"Of course not! I'd rather cut my stomach out first. Now pray continue. I want to hear what it was that drove you to such lengths."

Verena sank down into the proffered balloon-backed chair, feeling the prick of the red velvet through the thin muslin of her dress.

"My father is the Earl of Rosslyn and I ran away from an arranged marriage. I tried to buy a passage to France, where I once lived, but the only ship leaving that day was yours. I saw the notice and was told that you would not stand for a woman being on board, so I disguised myself as a simple chef and was hired."

The Marquis poured a glass of brandy and sipped it, his eyes never leaving her face.

"That accounts for the hair?"

"Yes, my Lord."

"Please, my name is James. We are equals. You are no longer a servant in my eyes and have no need to pay me a servant's respects. Please continue."

"That is all," Verena replied, bowing her head.

The Marquis leaned over to her and touched her lightly under the chin, bringing her face level with his.

"No, there is more, I can see it in your eyes. But you are frightened of telling me."

She could not help herself. Hot tears sprang onto her cheeks. She was overcome to feel the touch of his hand on her skin. Waves of affection washed over her and she was forced to look away.

"Please, I want to help you," said the Marquis gently. "You must be in great peril for you to feel such fear."

Verena could not help herself. She broke into sobs, her body shaking with the force of them.

"Lord Mountjoy attacked me and then held me prisoner in my own cabin. He is a friend of my stepmother and recognised me in spite of my disguise. He has threatened to send me back to England and a marriage I did not choose, if I do not comply with his demands."

"Which are?" enquired the Marquis, setting down his glass.

"I cannot say," whispered Verena, "they are too – too shocking."

"I am a man of the world. Nothing you can say would make me think less of you. If Lord Mountjoy has abused my hospitality, then I need to know of it."

The Marquis's expression was stern yet concerned.

Verena's voice was barely a whisper as she spoke, her eyes cast downwards in shame.

"He gave me the choice – either become his mistress and leave France for a life together in sin or if I did not choose that way, he would inform you of my deception and you would have me thrown in jail. He gave me until six o'clock to make my decision either way."

The Marquis's eyes glittered with anger. His mouth set into a hard thin line as he rose from the chair.

He strode across the polished floor of the Saloon, his hands behind his back, his face an unreadable mask. Verena could not bring herself to look at him as he paced hither and thither. At last, the Marquis spoke, "I want you to wait here, I will not be long."

"Where are you going?" she asked nervously. "I will be just outside on deck. I intend to apprehend this fellow myself." He strode purposefully towards the glass-etched door.

*

It was not long afterwards that Verena heard voices on the walkway outside. "Ah, just the person I want to see." It was Lord Mountjoy. "Jamie, old boy, we have a cuckoo in the nest."

"Oh?" replied the Marquis casually. Verena could only admire the cool and calm way in which he responded. It made her heart swell with love. "I should say! That chef of yours isn't quite all he seems."

"Really?" said the Marquis coolly. "Come into the Saloon, we do not want the crew to hear now, do we?" Confidently Lord Mountjoy swaggered into the room. He had the air of a man who believed he had won the day.

It wasn't until he saw Verena seated there in her fine white dress that he stopped short. For a few seconds, he appeared flustered and confused and then with admirable composure, he recovered himself.

"Ah, I see you have already apprehended our little impostor. Now, shall I go and fetch the *gendarmes* or will you send for the Steward?"

"There will be no *gendarmes* of any kind on the *Seahorse*," replied the Marquis coldly, as he closed the Saloon door. I think it is you who owes me an explanation, not Lady Verena."

Lord Mountjoy hesitated. His eyes darted from Verena to the Marquis and back again. She could see his mind whirling, attempting to come up with an explanation. She feared that he would talk himself out of trouble or that the Marquis would give in to him.

"Albert, I am waiting –"

The Marquis's tone was quite threatening as he snipped the end off a cigar and glared in Lord Mountjoy's direction.

"Look, Jamie, I don't know what this flibbertigibbet has told you, but it's a pack of lies. I found the hussy sneaking around the back streets of Marseilles, dressed as a boy. What would you think, old chap? A bit rum, eh, what?"

"I wonder what a spell in a Marseilles jail would do for your ability to tell the truth?" replied the Marquis, "if there is one thing I cannot abide, Albert, is a liar and a seducer. Add blackmail to the equation and it is not Lady Verena who is the wrongdoer here, but you.

"We have been friends for over twenty years and in that time I have forgiven your indiscretions and not heeded idle gossip about your morals. However, I now find them lacking and distasteful. I do not welcome men of dubious moral character onto the *Seahorse* to partake of my hospitality. I suggest that you leave this instant whilst I am still feeling well disposed.

"If you are still here by the time that dinner is served, I will indeed be sending the Steward out for the *gendarmes*, much as it would grieve me to do so, but it will not be to arrest Lady Verena. Do I make myself clear?"

Lord Mountjoy cast an evil look towards Verena, spitting with rage as he spoke,

"Do not think that I will fail to inform the Countess of your whereabouts the moment I return to the shore, madam. It will not be long before you are back in the bosom of your family."

The Marquis turned on him with a steely gaze.

"Be warned that from now on, Lady Verena is under my protection. She will not be taken anywhere against her will –"

Lord Mountjoy turned to leave the Saloon holding his head as high as he could, given that he was utterly defeated.

"Bad blood, that's what the Countess said. Hope you know what you're taking on, old boy!"

And with that, he departed.

There was an audible sigh of relief from Verena as the sound of Lord Mountjoy's footsteps retreated along the deck.

The Marquis struck a match and lit his cigar, sending up great clouds of scented smoke into the Saloon.

As he puffed, he fixed his stare on Verena. She trembled under the strength of his gaze, feeling that his eyes were penetrating her soul, reading her heart and her mind.

"That will be the last we see of him, I'll wager."

"But you have lost a friend and all on account of me."

The Marquis drew close to her, the smoke from his cigar wafting soft swirls upwards. Kneeling beside her chair, he gently pushed a lock of her hair away from her face.

"And now, young lady, as for you –"

Verena's heart swelled as he looked deep into her eyes.

CHAPTER NINE

The clear, blue sky of the Mediterranean wheeled overhead as the *Seahorse* steamed on through turquoise waters on a voyage of discovery and exploration.

On the bridge, Captain MacDonald steered the ship ever onwards, whilst below decks all was a hive of activity. It had just gone midday and in the galley preparations were well underway for luncheon.

The news had spread around the crew like wildfire about Lord Mountjoy's unceremonious departure from the vessel the previous evening. Some of the men had arrived back from an afternoon spent enjoying the delights of Marseilles in time to witness a dejected Lord Mountjoy hastily beating a retreat with his luggage thrown down the gangway after him.

Jack the cook had been more than astonished when he took his place in the galley later that evening to find that a comely young girl had replaced Jean. But still he did not soften his attitude towards her.

As Verena bustled around the galley preparing luncheon, he continued to scrutinise her every move, making loud comments when he thought that she was making an error.

"Don't think I'll be minding my language around you," he commented, chewing on a pencil, "you're in a man's world now and you'll just have to get used to it."

"I wouldn't expect you to behave in any other fashion," she had answered with a smile.

Verena cleaned and washed the salmon she had bought at the market the previous day and felt regret that she no longer had the big juicy scallops she had also purchased. In the scuffle with Lord Mountjoy, she had lost her basket containing most of her shopping.

"I never did get to taste those little boats," moaned Pete wistfully, as he entered the galley dragging a sack of salt behind him.

"I would not even mention them, if I were you," parried Verena sternly and then she began to laugh. Try as she might, she could not stay angry with the cheeky cabin boy for long.

"So, my Lady, I reckon it's all right for me to talk about what happened now?"

"I would wager that the whole crew are aware that Jean the chef is no more and that a lady is in his place," added Verena, as she poured olive oil into some egg yolks to make a special mayonnaise for the salmon.

As she worked, she hummed an air from Beethoven's *'Ode to Joy'*. It seemed a most suitable tune in the light of the previous evening's happenings.

Verena cast her mind back once more to the horrible moment when Lord Mountjoy had attempted to ruin her. It made her shudder to think that if the Marquis had not been such an honourable man and had been as much of a cad as his friend, she may well have found herself in a terrible situation.

'I feel as if Mama is still watching over me,' she thought as she stirred the mayonnaise one more time, 'my prayers have been answered. I left Rosslyn Hall knowing that there was something missing in my life and now I have found it in sweet James, the Marquis of Hilchester!'

She recalled with pleasure, how after Lord Mountjoy had been forcibly ejected from the *Seahorse*, the Marquis had sat with her for the remainder of the evening – listening intently as she recounted her tale.

He had produced many discs from the shelves of the Saloon and they had played every last one of them. Many were pieces that her mother used to play in happier times at Rosslyn Hall.

So lost in the music were they that neither of them had realised that the sky was beginning to grow lighter. They had talked until dawn.

With her heart full of hope, Verena had danced back to her cabin and snatched a few hours sleep before her day began in earnest.

Upon waking, the first object she had set eyes upon was the photograph of her beloved mother.

'Oh, Mama, the most wonderful thing has happened,' she whispered to the picture, 'I have fallen in love with the most dashing young gentleman. You would approve, he is the Marquis of Hilchester of a fine family with a country seat in Sussex and a house in Piccadilly. He is kind and brave, and oh, how I love him! He may not love me yet, but I intend to do everything in my power to make it so. Send me your blessing, Mama.'

And so, some six hours later, she was still full of hope and optimism that the promise for the future would hold good.

Arthur arrived in the galley ready to serve luncheon.

"Good afternoon, my Lady."

"Good afternoon, Arthur, I trust you are well this fine day?" Verena was bursting with happiness, her eyes shone and her expression was one of joy.

Arthur pointed at the pan containing the salmon.

"My Lady, I think your fish is starting to become rather well done?"

Verena rushed over the stove where the salmon was beginning to brown rapidly around the edges. She quickly folded a linen cloth into four and slid the pan off the heat.

"Goodness, it was half raw a moment ago! What must I have been thinking of?"

Arthur did not reply, he simply gave an enigmatic smile.

He had heard the music playing late into the night and early morning and had guessed that Verena had been with the Marquis all that time. In his heart, he was pleased. The Marquis had been on his own for too long – not a natural state of affairs for a young man, he thought.

"I hear we are sailing for Greece," remarked Verena. "I have long wished to visit Athens and all its glories."

"So I hear," replied Arthur, idly polishing a silver tray. "The Captain told me at breakfast this morning."

"I do hope I will be able to see the sights," she continued, dreamily. "The Parthenon, the cemetery at Kerameikos. I have a fancy to see where Lord Elgin found his famous marbles."

"Last I heard they were in the British Museum in London, my Lady."

Verena smiled at his sarcasm and forgave him. He had proved himself to be a true friend. When she had first set foot on the *Seahorse*, she would not have believed that she could have found such an ally.

But for Arthur's intervention, she may well have been on her way back to England and a desperately unhappy marriage.

"It's his Lordship's favourite peaches for pudding," said Verena, smiling, "Splendid," replied Arthur, "make sure there are some left for me. I dream of eating those almond-stuffed peaches."

As she began to clear up the dishes, Verena caught sight of herself in the polished surface of a silver tray.

She picked it up and peered at her distorted reflection. She felt sad that the Marquis had not seen her with her glorious long hair, but last night he had made kind comments about her shorn locks.

As she had left the Saloon to retire for the night, he had gently touched the top of her head saying, "Don't worry, it will soon grow back but I think that short hair becomes your loveliness even more."

She had blushed deeply and modestly cast her eyes downwards. The touch of his fingertips had sent shocks along her spine. She felt wonderfully alive and it kindled hope in her heart that the Marquis could fall in love with her, as she was with him.

And now, they were on their way to Greece! Home of her beloved Gods and Goddesses.

She felt quite sure that the islands and Athens would weave their spell and bring the pair of them close together.

'Who could fail to fall in love in that atmosphere?' she thought, as she slid the stuffed peaches onto a glass dish.

Everything she had cooked today was completed with more than her usual care and attention. She wanted to woo the Marquis with her fine cuisine, lovingly prepared. She wanted to show him what a wonderful wife she would make –

'But I am being premature,' she scolded herself, 'I must not tempt fate by thinking such thoughts.'

Even so, she went about her duties for the rest of the day in a complete dream.

*

And so Lady Verena soon found that she fell into a routine with the Marquis.

Each day she would prepare breakfast and then luncheon. Next she would rest or read as the Marquis had allowed her access to his library.

After dinner, she would wait anxiously to be invited into the Saloon where they would spend the rest of the evening discussing everything from Greek legends to the Marquis's various archaeological expeditions.

One evening, he took out a gold torque bracelet and placed it around Verena's slender wrist – it fitted her perfectly.

"It is as if it was made for you," he declared, his amber eyes burning into her hers with a fervent intensity.

Verena tilted her face upwards, hoping that their lips would meet – but to no avail.

Even though the Marquis was most solicitous and showered her with compliments, the final confirmation of love was sadly lacking.

'There is plenty of time,' she told herself one evening as she hurried along the deck to the Saloon, 'we still have at least three days sailing before we arrive in Athens. As Arthur has said, he is not used to female company.'

The evening began well. The Marquis had allowed her to choose a disc to be played on the gramophone and as the last few notes sounded, he became strangely thoughtful.

"There is one thing I do not understand," he said at last, "and that is why your father married Lady Louisa in the first place. You say that he was in unremitting mourning for quite some years after your mother died, yet this marriage of his seems so sudden and without thought."

Verena sighed and straightened her gown.

"It is true, one day he sent for me and informed me that he was to visit London on business. He said that he was to be gone for almost a month – which was quite unusual – but as he was visiting my aunt, Lady Armstrong, and her husband has been ill for many months, I thought that maybe it was family business that made him linger."

"But then he arrived home with a new wife, you say?"

As the Marquis drew closer, she could feel his breath upon her skin and it sent waves of delight throughout her whole being.

"Yes, it was most unexpected. We had received hardly any news of him for quite some weeks, apart from a few brief notes, and none that presaged his arrival back at Rosslyn Hall. He appeared one day whilst I was out riding and I was shocked to find that he was not alone."

She paused, clearly reliving the emotions of that day.

"I arrived back at Rosslyn Hall and proceeded straight to the drawing room. I was in a most dishevelled state. Jet, my mount, had taken me through the old quarry and I was covered from head to foot in dust.

"I was deeply shocked to be told that the strange woman who sat with him, Lady Louisa Middleton-Jones, was my new stepmother. Not that Papa should consult me before marrying of course, but I had thought that he might have at least written and told me."

"It sounds to me like this marriage was a business deal. I have come across many such transactions in London society. They say that the age of the arranged marriages is dead, but let me tell you, my dear, there are many bought and sold over the gaming tables of Mayfair!"

Verena looked at him, quite taken aback. The Marquis was wearing a strange expression.

"James, I do not think that Papa bargained for my stepmother over a game of cards!" she exclaimed.

"No, no, I meant no ill by that remark," the Marquis replied, "I simply refer to the fact that we dutiful sons and daughters are sometimes but pawns in the game of life. But tell me, I wish to know more about this marriage that the Countess attempted to foist upon you. Had you no warning?"

"None whatsoever. The matter was broached over dinner one evening. At first it was presented to me as a choice. But as the meal wore on, it became quite apparent that the deal had already been brokered."

"And the man she selected as your intended?"

Verena shuddered.

"The Duke of Dalkenneth. I do not know if you have made his acquaintance, but he comes from Scotland. His first wife died, leaving no issue – a most unfortunate situation for man in his forties. And so he sought to rectify this turn of events by approaching the Countess for my hand in marriage.

She had met him at one of her London *soirées* and he had mentioned that he was searching for a suitable wife. The Countess leapt at the opportunity and I was to have no say in the matter."

"I have nearly fallen foul of such schemes myself," murmured the Marquis, darkly.

He paused and looked into the distance.

"My father, on his very deathbed, expressed his concern at what he construed as my lack of willingness to wed. But I refused to be traded like a bullock in a market. He died reproaching me for it."

Verena's blood suddenly ran cold. As she searched the Marquis's handsome face for some sign of warmth, she looked and found none. She was not sure that this conversation was proceeding in quite the way she would have liked.

"And do you still find it necessary to avoid such a union, James?" she asked, fearful of the reply.

Her hands were trembling in the long seconds that ticked by without a response from the Marquis. Then suddenly he stood up, his manner at once cold and distant.

"If you will forgive me, madam, I am quite tired this evening. The meal was excellent as always, but I find myself in need of an early night. I bid you good evening."

Verena slowly arose from her chair, feeling utterly disheartened.

"Good night, James," she said stiffly as he left the Saloon.

Wandering along the deck, she could not help but feel the grip of panic fastening itself around her heart. Why had the Marquis become so cool towards her? It was a valid enough question. He had made enquiries of a far more personal nature over these past few evenings and she had not flinched from any of them.

'I have touched a raw nerve,' she thought, as she paced the deck.

She was far from sleepy and this unsettling turn of events had upset her deeply.

'But why did he react so when I mentioned marriage?' She wandered along the deck for some time, watching the pitching waves and the twinkling stars overhead before retiring.

But sleep would not come. She tossed in her hard bunk for hours before finally closing her eyes.

*

The next few evenings the Marquis failed to request her presence in the Saloon after dinner. By the third evening Verena was beside herself.

'What is this secret that he holds so close to his chest?' she wondered, as she retired to her cabin each night after the evening meal had been cleared away.

'Why does he find the idea of marriage so repugnant?' She considered asking Arthur, but a sense of propriety prevented her from doing so. Even though he had become a friend, she could not ask him something so intimate. As Jean, she may have ventured such a question, but as Lady Verena, it was unthinkable.

The next day dawned and on the horizon the fair City of Athens was visible.

Before she made breakfast, Verena climbed up on deck and watched as the ship steamed slowly into the harbour.

In her dreams she had imagined that she and the Marquis would be standing side-by-side for this momentous occasion, but instead she found herself alongside Pete as the *Seahorse* made its approach.

The ship eventually dropped anchor in the bay, so with a sigh Verena returned below decks to prepare breakfast.

Supplies were now running low as they had been at sea nearly a week, so she made kedgeree with some leftover fish and garnished it with a few hard-boiled eggs.

It was with a heavy heart that she picked at the food that Jack had made for her and the rest of the crew. She could hear the men shouting in the mess next door. They were relieved to be on extended shore leave – the Marquis had told them they were docking for at least two if not three days.

Verena had been hoping that she would be spending that time alone with the Marquis. He had promised to show her places that the tourists did not visit. Amongst his many accomplishments he also spoke Greek and she had been looking forward to visiting some Athenians in their own environment.

'Alas, that will not happen now,' she sighed, stacking the dishes in the sink.

"Erhem," came a coughing noise behind her.

She whirled round to see the Marquis standing in the doorway of the galley, his hand just covering his mouth.

"Ah, Verena, I want you to come on a trip with me," he said refusing to meet her eyes, "there is something I wish to show you."

Her heart leapt, this is what she had longed to hear. Her spirits soared for an instant and then she composed herself.

This intriguing offer may not be what she imagined.

"I would like that very much, my Lord," she replied formally.

"Good."

The Marquis appeared quite awkward, so unlike how he had been with her during their long evenings together.

"The ferry to the shore will leave in twenty minutes. I suggest you take some kind of head-covering with you – we may be visiting Churches where to go bare-headed would cause offence to the local people."

"Naturally," replied Verena.

She wanted to skip and dance, but still smarting from the Marquis's rebuff, she did not allow herself the luxury of indulging her emotions.

Back in her cabin she changed into her white muslin dress and pulled a thin scarf from her luggage.

'I am in desperate need of some new clothes,' she said to herself, 'I must take some money with me in case there are any shops or dressmakers. If we are here for a few days then I could easily get something run up.'

She counted out some coins and a few pound notes, which she folded tightly into her black silk bag. She was certain that the Marquis would know where she could change her money into drachmas – there would surely be a bank nearby.

When she emerged on deck, the Marquis was already waiting by the harness.

"I am afraid we will have to swing you over the side and lower you to the boat," he said gruffly.

Two of the crew helped Verena into the harness. She sat nervously on the thin plank that constituted the seat and held her breath.

"Mind how you go now, my Lady," shouted one of the men, as he winched the harness up and over the side.

Verena could not look as the harness descended slowly. She fixed her gaze on the Parthenon while she slowly shuddered downwards.

"Take care, my Lady!" came the cry from the waiting boat.

Verena came to her senses as the man steadied the harness and unclipped her.

Stepping gingerly onto the moving boat, she let out a cry as her foot slipped on the wet wood.

"Verena, are you all right?" called the Marquis from up on deck.

"Yes, I am, thank you."

A few minutes later, the Marquis was lowered onto the waiting ferry. He stepped neatly out of the harness to join her.

"Ready to go, my Lord?" enquired the seaman on board.

The Marquis nodded his assent and the man began to row towards the shore.

They made the journey in complete silence. Verena was longing to ask him what it was that he so urgently wanted to show her, but she found she could not.

Stepping ashore onto a little jetty, Verena walked on ahead, anxious to stand on Greek soil.

The Acropolis rose magnificently in front of her. The sun blazed down as she shielded her eyes to gain a better view.

"We will make our way to the Parthenon first," explained the Marquis as they walked towards the hill, "and from there, we will proceed to Kerameikos. There is also a wonderful museum full of artefacts that I wish to see after lunch. I think you will enjoy seeing their fine collection of statues."

Verena's heart ached as the Marquis walked alongside her, so stiff and formal. She could sense that he was not at all relaxed.

The Parthenon was everything she had imagined and more. The Marquis was incredibly knowledgeable about the site and pointed out where Lord Elgin had chipped off the famous marbles.

They took a carriage to the cemetery of Kerameikos and she was entranced by the ancient graves.

"Now for some luncheon," declared the Marquis, as they picked their way over broken gravestones. "I know a most agreeable *taverna* back down in the town."

Ever the gentleman, he helped Verena up into the waiting carriage. It was open and had no canopy to speak of. The sun was so fierce overhead that it hurt Verena's eyes.

It was not an easy ride – the driver seemed to pay no heed to the carts and animals that wandered into the road in front of him, and more than once he waved his arms shouting in Greek at the poor unfortunate who got in his way.

By the time they reached their destination, Verena was feeling quite faint. She was unaccustomed to such heat – even though she had visited the South of France in summer, but that was nothing compared to here in Athens.

"I am afraid we will have to walk for a while," said the Marquis, "the *taverna* is concealed up a back street and although it is not that far from here, it is inaccessible for the horses."

Verena stepped down from the carriage feeling most unwell. As she waited in the soaring heat for the Marquis to finish his parley with the driver, she was suddenly overcome with dizziness.

Before she knew it, she had collapsed in a heap on the cobbles outside a jewellery shop.

"*Verena*," cried the Marquis, as she sank to the floor.

In a stream of Greek, he entreated the driver to help him move her into the cool of the shop.

An old man with white hair and a bushy moustache was sitting outside on a wooden chair. He immediately stood up and gestured to the Marquis to place Verena on it.

"Please, some water," he called in Greek.

The old man shuffled inside the shop. Very soon a crowd was gathering to witness the event.

After some minutes an old lady dressed entirely in black peasant clothes came out of the shop carrying a tray with a jug of water and a glass.

"Drink, drink," she exhorted in broken English.

As the old woman wetted Verena's parched lips, she gradually came to.

During the commotion, Verena had let go of her black silk bag and it lay at her feet.

In a flash, an unseen hand snatched the bag from the floor and a shout went up from the crowd.

"Thief, thief!"

"Please, look after the lady – I will return," ordered the Marquis, "Do not chase them," the old man said in Greek, waving his arms, "they are dangerous men, they will kill you!"

Without a second's hesitation, the Marquis sped through the crowd after the thief.

"What happened?" mumbled Verena, coming to at last. "Where am I?"

The old Greek lady patted her hand and gesticulated at the Marquis's rapidly disappearing broad back.

In her daze, Verena could not understand what the lady was saying to her.

"I am sorry, I do not understand. Oh, where is the Marquis? James, James. Where are you?"

"We wait, you see," said the old man. His command of English was tenuous but there was no doubting the kindness of his heart.

In rapid Greek, he spoke to the old lady, his wife, who tottered into the shop.

Five minutes later, she reappeared with a plate of pastries and sweetmeats. She gestured to Verena to eat. Absent-mindedly choosing a sticky confection full of nuts,

Verena put it in her mouth and chewed without really tasting what she was eating.

Where had the Marquis gone? What was he thinking of, running after some rough Greek fellow who, for all he knew, may have a knife?

The kindly shopkeepers fanned her and offered her endless pastries and glasses of water.

After half an hour, the old lady produced some thick bitter coffee that was a welcome change from the sweetness of the pastries.

All around her, people were talking animatedly – but she could not understand a word.

As time wore on and the Marquis did not reappear, Verena became more and more anxious.

Her worst fears were confirmed when the crowd parted to admit a tall man in uniform, accompanied by a handful of surly looking colleagues.

"Lady Verena Rosslyn?" the tall man spoke perfect English but laced with a thick, Greek accent.

"Yes?"

"I think you should come with me to the British Consulate. You will be quite safe there."

"But the Marquis?" she asked, her brow furrowed with worry.

"He is at the Consulate – now if you would be so kind?"

He gestured towards a waiting carriage.

Verena barely had time to thank the kind shopkeepers before she was escorted to the carriage.

As they sped through the streets of Athens, no one spoke.

'I pray that James is safe,' she thought, anxiously. 'He has to be safe. Oh, what will I do without him if the worst has happened? I cannot bear to even consider it.' Verena found that she could not enjoy her ride through the streets of Athens.

All about her life carried on, but a part of her had ceased to exist until she knew that the Marquis was safe.

The carriage finally halted outside a tall white building with heavily shuttered windows.

The official helped her down onto the street and waited whilst his colleagues climbed out.

"This way, please, my Lady."

He led her through a magnificent, mosaic-floored entrance hall. All around rose tall Grecian pillars carved from marble and on the walls were many fine paintings.

She was taken through into an adjoining room. The man beckoned her to sit down on one of the brown leather sofas, so like the ones at Rosslyn Hall, and left her alone.

Anxious moments ticked by until finally the doors opened and in strode a small neat man with grey hair wearing pinstripe trousers and a close-cut jacket.

Verena admired his style, so fashionable back in London, but she had not expected to encounter such sartorial elegance in this far-flung corner of the Mediterranean.

"My Lady? I am Sir Richard Wells, Ambassador of Her Majesty's Government. Would you be so kind as to follow me?"

"The Marquis?" she entreated, her voice rising.

"Come with me and you will be reunited."

With bated breath, Verena followed Sir Richard.

"How do you find Athens?"

"A trifle hot and dangerous so far."

The Ambassador nodded sagely, "Yes, we have problems with an itinerate population, mainly from the islands, but thankfully no one has died as yet."

"Then the Marquis is safe?"

Sir Richard opened a pair of white doors and there – seated on a wooden chair, his head bandaged and a cut on his hand being cleaned by the attending doctor – was the Marquis.

"*James*," she cried, casting aside all composure and running to his side. "I was frantic with worry."

The Marquis dived into his coat pocket and brought out a very crumpled black silk bag.

"I am afraid I couldn't wrestle the contents off the bounders."

Verena crushed the bag to her chest.

"I am not concerned about losing my money, I just feared for your life."

"A bump on the head and a cut where the fellow tried to bite me – apart from that, I am quite fit and well. The worst thing is that you missed the lunch I promised you and I failed to show you what I had expressly wanted you to see."

"Another time, another time," said Verena, soothingly. She could not resist the temptation to rest her hand upon his. It was warm and reassuring.

"Now, if this kind doctor will allow me, let us resume our tour. Doctor?"

"I would advise rest, my Lord, but I can see no harm to a little light walking."

The Marquis looked at Verena and his eyes were resolute.

"Verena, will you be so good as to accompany me?"

"Of course, but only if you are feeling quite well enough," she replied, thrilled at the opportunity.

"Then, come. We have tarried long enough. Sir Richard, I cannot thank you sufficiently for your help. I will call again before we leave."

Without further ado, the Marquis shook the Ambassador's hand firmly before striding towards the door.

Verena followed him all the while gazing up at him in mute adoration.

'What is it that he wishes to show me that means so much to him?' she wondered, as they left the cool of the Consulate to step outside into the sticky Athens afternoon. 'This is a rare puzzle indeed!'

Barely pausing to find his bearings, the Marquis took her by the hand and led her purposefully through the streets.

CHAPTER TEN

Verena was grateful that the staff at the Consulate had given her a flask of fresh water, for as she and the Marquis trudged up the long dusty streets, she soon became thirsty.

The road seemed to lead forever upwards and although the sun was now dipping in the sky, its heat was still incredibly fierce.

"Is it much further?" she gasped, stopping to take a sip of water.

They were in a narrow street full of square-built white dwellings – they looked as if they were staggering up the hill in a jumble.

"Do you need to rest awhile?" asked the Marquis. Although he had taken off his jacket, he seemed quite at home in the soaring temperature.

Whilst Verena felt certain that her face was red and unattractive, the Marquis looked as if he had just stepped off the *Seahorse* after a bracing trip round the bay.

"It is just that this incline is quite steep and the heat is defeating me," replied Verena, feeling more than a little dizzy again.

"There is a clearing with some trees and a bench ahead," said the Marquis. "If you can make it up there, we can rest awhile. It is not much further on after that, I promise."

Verena gathered herself together and renewed her assault on the steep hill ahead.

She was almost bent double when, some minutes later, they eventually arrived at a cool-looking clearing. There, as the Marquis had promised, was a modest wooden bench.

Verena caught her breath at the magnificent view over the City.

"This is simply marvellous," she cried, sitting down under the shade of an olive tree, scanning the vista across the Bay of Athens.

"It makes the climb well worth it," remarked the Marquis, striding to the edge of the clearing and taking in the full panorama.

"Won't you tell me where we are going?" implored Verena, "You will see," was all the Marquis would say.

They sat there for some fifteen minutes enjoying the shade. Verena stretched up and pulled a ripe olive off a branch.

"Oh, but it isn't anything like the olives I have bought in markets," she observed, looking at the strange-coloured fruit.

"That is because olives are dried and cured before they are sold," explained the Marquis. "In this state, you cannot eat them – they are far too bitter. Now, come, let us resume our walk."

Reluctantly, Verena arose from the wooden bench and left the cool of the clearing for the hot dusty road.

It seemed to go on forever. Eventually they were nearly on the same level as the Acropolis.

At last, as they reached the outskirts of Athens, a beautiful Church came into view.

'My goodness,' she thought, excitedly, 'surely he is not going to spring a surprise on me and we are to be wed!' Her thoughts were whirling as they climbed the last few steps towards the Church.

"Byzantine?" enquired Verena, "Without doubt," replied the Marquis taking her by the hand.

At the feel of his fingers, Verena suddenly quivered in anticipation. Apart from the occasional light touch on the head or arm, he had not initiated such close contact before.

She felt awkward and uncomfortable.

'How can this be when it is what I have longed for?' she thought, her heart racing. He led her across the flagstones towards the heavy oak entrance.

'Are we going inside? What are his intentions?' However, instead of walking into the cool interior, the Marquis abruptly changed direction and followed the path alongside the Church.

"A fine example of eleventh century architecture," he declared, waving his hand at the narrow windows.

But Verena could hear in his voice that he was not quite as composed as he appeared.

As they followed the path, it opened out into a small churchyard. Without saying a word, he began to pick his away around the headstones, dragging Verena behind him.

Suddenly they came to a halt by a simple stone memorial that read,

'My dearest beloved – 1839-1872
Always in our hearts'

Verena stared and stared at the stone in utter incomprehension. Who was buried here? And why was he or she so important to the Marquis?

'Well, I haven't come all this way to look at an anonymous tomb,' she fumed to herself irritably, now feeling quite exhausted from her exertions.

Turning to the Marquis, intending to air her complaint, she was shocked to see that tears were welling up in his eyes.

His head was bent in sorrow and his whole body appeared limp with grief.

Verena instantly felt remorseful. Whoever it was who lay buried here had to be someone of importance to the Marquis.

But who could it be in this hidden corner of Athens, so far away from home?

Slowly the realisation came to her. The Marquis had never mentioned his mother.

Verena gently touched him on the arm and said in a tender whisper, "I am not the only motherless child, am I?"

The Marquis shook his head and slowly sank to his knees. In a voice choked with emotion, he began to speak,

"I was just seven years of age. My father and mother loved to sail – we owned a fine clipper in those days, the fastest in the whole Mediterranean. One summer, we were sailing around the Greek Islands and we stopped over at Athens intending to linger awhile and visit friends. It had been a far hotter summer that year than usual and it was rumoured that there was an outbreak of typhoid in the City.

"I was too young to understand what that meant. One day I was outside playing with my little Greek friends, when I noticed some older boys throwing stones at a kitten. I ran over to them and shouted at them to stop. I think they were surprised to see this pale English boy yelling and looking rather threatening, so they left it alone.

"I took the kitten indoors and looked after it. A week or so later, it died. I was beside myself, but then my mother suddenly fell ill with a raging fever. She, too, died a few days later.

"I thought I was to blame because I had overheard one of the servants saying that it was the kitten that had brought disease into the house. For years I walked around with the guilt of it."

"But surely it was not your fault?" asked Verena softly.

The Marquis wiped his tears with his handkerchief trying hard to regain his composure.

"Yes, I know that now. But my father did not make it any easier for me. He was too wrapped up in his own grief to give me any reassurances. He loved my mother till his dying day and looked at no other. He had her buried here because she had loved the City so much."

There was a long silence. Verena gently touched the Marquis's elbow to let him know that she cared and then walked a few paces away so that he might be alone to pay his respects.

As she stood in the little churchyard, how she longed to run over to him and throw her arms around him.

'But I cannot, it would not be appropriate,' she told herself sadly.

She understood now why sometimes he behaved in a strange offhand manner. He was alone in the world. Had he not said that his father had only died the previous year? Why, he was barely out of mourning, what could she expect?

'I must tread gently,' she resolved, 'this is not a man to be rushed. I must be prepared to wait for as long as it takes.' The Marquis walked towards her, his whole bearing and expression so much softer than it had been.

"Come, you must be famished. I am sure that if we go down into the town we will find a morsel to eat."

He looked right into Verena's eyes as he spoke and she sensed that there was now a new understanding between them.

He took her hand once more and led her out of the churchyard without a backwards glance.

*

Arriving back on board the *Seahorse*, there was a surprise awaiting Verena.

"My Lady, if you please, there are some packages that have been delivered for you. They are on the bridge with the Captain."

Arthur had met her straight off the ferry. She was barely out of the harness before he was at her elbow, eager to relay the news.

"What kind of packages, Arthur?" she enquired most intrigued.

"I could not say, my Lady. They arrived whilst you were out with his Lordship."

Piqued with curiosity, Verena made her way to the bridge where Captain MacDonald was poring over some maps.

"Ah, my Lady, I expect you've come for your parcels? I did not think that you had had time for shopping –"

"You are quite right, I haven't," she replied, pulling at the string on the uppermost box in the pile. "I am utterly mystified."

She did not wait. She tore off the string, pulled open the lid and gasped in amazement.

"How beautiful," she cried, taking out a cream linen gown.

She opened up the remainder of the boxes to find a pair of summer slippers, a fine linen skirt in navy and a white blouse covered in *broderie anglaise*.

"But this is most strange, I have not been shopping today. There has been no time. We had such a horrible experience on the streets of Athens. I fainted and then my bag was snatched. So as you can see, it is not I who has been extravagant."

"No, they are gifts from me."

Verena turned to find that the Marquis was standing behind her.

"As soon as you revealed yourself to me, I took the liberty of wiring the British Consulate and ordering some clothes for you. The Ambassador's wife was most helpful – she has exquisite taste as you can see. I am afraid I guessed your size. I hope they will fit you."

Verena held the white blouse against her, thrilled at something new to wear.

"I will go below and try them on at once and thank you, thank you so much. You must allow me to pay you for them."

"As I have said, they are gifts and I will not hear of such a thing. But please, do me the honour of wearing the cream

162

dress this evening. I trust you will be joining me after dinner for some conversation and music?"

Verena was bursting with joy, her heart felt so full of love that she was almost swooning.

"I will be there, James," she whispered, looking up at him adoringly.

"Excellent," he said with a smile, "I am looking forward to an enjoyable evening."

*

By the time that Verena had returned to her cabin to put away her new clothes, it was getting on for half past six.

'Goodness! I have to begin dinner.' She did not have time to change. She simply rushed towards the galley. Upon entering, she could see that Arthur was already beginning his preparations.

"You're running late," he commented, putting down the silver polish and a candelabrum.

"Heavens, I did not realise how late it was. I have had an exhausting day. Now let me see, the Marquis will not be requiring three courses this evening, we ate late this afternoon."

Arthur raised an eyebrow but said nothing.

Verena continued, "It was in a delightful little *taverna*, tucked away in a back street. I had the most heavenly *dolmades* and a chickpea puree with little flat breads –"

"Dol-what?" enquired Arthur, "*Dolmades* – vine leaves stuffed with rice and herbs. Quite unusual, I may try and make them myself and I think they would be quite easy."

"That reminds me, you recall the list you sent Pete off with to go shopping?"

Verena hesitated. In her haste to enjoy her time with the Marquis, she had entrusted Pete with the task of restocking her supplies. She had the most awful feeling that Arthur was about to tell her that he had forgotten.

"You will not believe this, but the boy came back with every last item."

Verena heaved a sigh of relief, "I thought you were about to tell me that he had not bought a single thing!"

"Don't worry, my Lady. I made it quite plain what would happen to the rest of his shore leave should he fail."

"Thank you so much, Arthur. What would I do without you?"

"Well, my Lady, by the grace of God I will be in the Marquis's employ for a very long time to come."

"I'll say Amen to that!"

They were still laughing as Verena ventured into the store cupboard – it was completely full again. There were bowls of big fat tomatoes still on the vine, a crate of lemons, peaches, jars of kalamata olives, bunches of fresh mint, marjoram and thyme –

"Oh, what is this?" she quizzed, opening a sack of an unfamiliar-looking grain. "The label says 'pourgouri'."

Arthur peered into the sack and grimaced,

"Looks like that horrible stuff they serve you in Africa. I would wager that is the Greek version of it."

Verena remembered a dish she had seen in the *taverna* that looked as if it had been made with the same grain. She had noticed that it had been dressed with lemon juice and mint.

"Have no fear, Arthur, by the time I have finished you will not recognise it."

Dipping a jug into the sack, she soon had the contents steaming over a pan of boiling water.

"Now, I will chop some tomatoes, add lemon juice and mint and it will make a fine accompaniment to the main course. I do hope that Pete found me a decent spring lamb."

It was to be a simple dish – grilled lamb, cooked in the Greek style, served with *pommes de terre en blanquette* and fine beans.

Diving back into the store cupboard, she brought out some eggs, flour, sugar, butter and a couple of lemons.

"I think a nice lemon sponge will be the perfect way to end the meal – I want it to be lemony, moist and as light as a feather."

Arthur beat the eggs for her whilst she creamed the butter and sugar together. She then zested two of the lemons in the grater.

"So did you discover who sent those mysterious packages that appeared this afternoon?" asked Arthur, as he tipped the beaten eggs into Verena's bowl.

Verena could feel herself blushing deeply – she did not want to answer him.

"Ah, I see – " said Arthur knowingly.

She was praying that something would rescue her from the ensuing awkward silence – and a potentially embarrassing explanation – when all of a sudden there came a massive roaring sound from beneath their feet.

"Goodness, what is that?" exclaimed Verena.

"It sounds like the ship's engines, my Lady."

"But surely it cannot be?"

Just then, the *Seahorse* gave an enormous lurch – so violent that Verena dropped her wooden spoon onto the floor of the galley.

"We are moving," she called, "Arthur, do run upstairs and find out what is happening. This lamb is at a crucial stage and I cannot leave it. I would hate to serve the Marquis a burnt offering."

"Right away, my Lady," replied Arthur, springing up from his seat.

Alone in the galley, Verena wondered what had made the Marquis change his plans.

'We were not due to leave Athens until the day after tomorrow. Why has our stay been cut short? The crew will be most unhappy.' The door to the galley opened and Arthur returned.

She looked at him expectantly.

"Well?"

"It seems that the Marquis has ordered the ship to sail at once, my Lady. The Captain did not know why and did not feel that it was his place to query his orders."

"Of course," murmured Verena, "but it does seem a rather sudden decision."

She returned to basting the lamb. Now she could not wait until after dinner to find out for herself the reason for this unexpected departure.

Fifteen minutes later the dinner was served.

Verena waited anxiously for the meal to end. By the time that Jack had appeared, she was really feeling quite nervous.

"Do you know why we have left Athens so early?" she asked.

"No, I don't and I'm not happy about it," barked Jack, "I was planning to spend tonight in a nice little *taverna* and now I'm stuck here. Hmmph!"

Verena resumed icing the lemon sponge – she placed little curls of lemon peel on top and drizzled the whole cake with sugar syrup.

"There that should sweeten the proceedings," she declared as she slid it onto a bone china plate.

Jack made a disgruntled noise and began to clang pots and pans around the galley.

'I will be glad to take my leave of this place tonight,' she thought, 'now I must run to my cabin and put on my new dress.' She loaded the cake onto the dumb waiter and sent it upstairs with one tug of the rope.

"You're not stopping for dinner?" asked Jack, in a surly fashion.

"No, I am not hungry," replied Verena truthfully.

"More for me then."

Verena cast her eyes upwards in exasperation. There were now very few unpleasant things about being on board the *Seahorse,* but Jack was definitely one of them.

In spite of the Marquis expressly requesting her presence in the Saloon after dinner, Verena felt quite wary.

'I must not expect too much, in case his mood has changed once again,' she told herself as she put on her elegant new dress and matching slippers.

She brushed her hair till it shone and pinched her cheeks. Catching sight of herself in her tiny mirror, she could see that the expression she wore was one of anxiety rather than joyous anticipation.

With a wildly beating heart Verena made her way to the Saloon. She hesitated outside the doors before knocking – inside she could hear the gramophone was playing Beethoven's '*Moonlight Sonata*'. '

The perfect setting for romance,' she mused and then sighed heavily.

Apart from a few meaningful stares and the fact that he had held her hand that afternoon, the Marquis had shown no inclination of affection towards her.

'But I have vowed to be patient,' she reminded herself, 'and I am determined to wait, even if it takes another hundred voyages around the Mediterranean.'

Composing herself she waited until the music had died away before knocking.

But the seconds ticked by and the Marquis did not bid her enter.

'Perhaps he has forgotten that he has invited me,' she wondered or maybe he is ignoring me.'

She was on the point of leaving, when the door flew open, "Verena, my dear. Do come in."

'This is unusual,' she thought, 'he has not done this before.' "Might I say how beautiful you look this evening, Verena?"

Compliments! She was quite taken aback by his effusiveness.

"Now, please be seated, I have much to talk to you about."

He took her by the hand and led her to a chaise. Verena sank down, unsure of how to interpret his behaviour.

There was a long pause before he spoke, "I feel that I owe you an explanation for my recent conduct –"

"Really, James, there is no need. I understand that you have been through an enormous amount and it all became much clearer to me today."

"Please, let me continue –"

He gazed deep into her eyes, his expression both entreating and earnest.

"Dearest Verena, there is so much I have wanted to say to you, but I have struggled with myself over how to begin."

She could feel the blood rising to her cheeks as she listened. She remained silent, scarcely daring to breathe in case she missed a single word.

"In the days since I discovered your true identity, I have found myself to be overwhelmed by my feelings for you. Verena, my darling, *do you understand what I am saying*?"

He sat down on the chaise next to her and took her hand gently in his own.

She wanted to answer him, but could not speak.

"My darling, there is still a part of me that is convinced that anyone or anything I love is destined to die. It is as if my love was a poison that can only kill. When I first saw you as your true wonderful self, I found myself in utter turmoil.

After that long evening together, I was terrified by my feelings.

"Then today, standing by my mother's grave, I knew that I had to reveal my love for you. Darling, could you love me?"

"Oh, yes, *yes*!" cried Verena, her eyes shining.

The Marquis kissed her hand with fervour and then gently met her lips with his.

Verena was filled with joy in one instant – *he loved her*!

His kisses became more persistent and demanding and she felt that she was floating away on a cloud of sheer joy.

He held her in his arms for what seemed like an eternity before releasing her. His warm amber eyes were so full of love that it made her heart feel like bursting.

"It was as if I had to take you to where my mother is buried to make sure of my emotions. I now know I was right and I believe that she has been guiding me towards blissful happiness."

They remained locked in an embrace for long moments and then Verena reluctantly pulled free.

"But why have we left Athens? I had expected that we might stay a little longer – there is still so much to see. Please do not tell me that we are returning to England. Even though I now feel so much stronger, knowing I have your love, but I do not think I could bear it."

"Please, worry no more. We are not bound for England but Cyprus, the birthplace of Aphrodite. I have a very special reason for wishing us to curtail our visit to Athens."

Verena looked at him, searching his amber eyes for some clue. His smile was so warm and gentle – and it was a smile just for her.

The Marquis stood up and sank to his knees at her feet.

"Verena, my darling, there is the most wonderful little Church in Limassol – it has so many wonderful memories for me – and I want so much to take you there."

"I would love to," she whispered feeling that she must be in a dream to be this happy.

"And there, I wish that you would do me the honour of becoming my wife. The priest is an old family friend and he will conduct the service, if you will only say yes. Do say *yes*, my darling, I beg of you!"

Verena's eyes filled with tears. Such happiness!

"My life is now complete," she murmured. "Yes, James, of course I will marry you in Limassol."

"Oh, my dearest Verena, I am the happiest man alive," cried the Marquis. "There is no other way I would wish to spend the rest of my life than by your side."

"And I will always love you with all my body and soul forever and ever."

"Verena, we will be *so* happy together."

"And returning to England?" she muttered, "what of that?"

"If you do not wish to go home, there is no reason why we cannot stay on the *Seahorse* a while longer. Is there anything that requires your immediate attention in England?"

Verena thought hard. Her father. Much as he had hurt her, she still loved him dearly and missed him. And she was sure that he felt the same way.

The Countess could not come between father and daughter for too long – "There is Papa," she answered, "I need to make my peace with him and explain why I ran away."

"Surely he will forgive you? How could anyone not," exclaimed the Marquis, holding her closely once again.

Verena considered awhile.

"He has his life with the Countess and now I have mine. I am sure he would approve of you, once he has recovered from the shock.

"I feel so very loved, James, with you I can face anything – even the Countess. I love you so very much from the very depths of my heart."

The Marquis kissed her passionately and stroked her hair, his eyes so full of love.

"Darling, together we can do anything. We are sailing to the very *Heart of Love* – you and I are just beginning our journey through life. Together forever!"

They held each other so closely that they felt that they were one.

The *Seahorse* continued to carry them through sparkling blue waters towards their destination, where they would receive the blessings of Aphrodite and all the ancient Gods and Goddesses for their true love which will last for as long as time itself.

Printed in Poland
by Amazon Fulfillment
Poland Sp. z o.o., Wrocław